A

"It was no a   have a feeling
things look sin   ould dust the
place for fingerprints."

Nick's midnight-black eyes bulged in disbelief. "You want me to *dust* the *garden?* No way, Hazard. Your weird suspicions have led you astray on this particular case," he assured her. "Sheila obviously climbed the ladder to repair the antenna so she could watch her favorite soap opera. She was startled by the wasps under the eave, and maybe even stung. When she fell, she landed on the picket fence and then plunged into the melons. End of story."

Amanda disagreed. "The murderer left the rake in the garden."

"The *rake,*" Nick repeated dubiously.

"Whoever shoved Sheila raked over the incriminating footprints and didn't replace the tool in Lula MacAdo's alphabetically organized shed."

Nick groaned. "Hell's bells, Hazard, how do you come up with this stuff?"

Amanda gnashed her teeth, reminding herself that Thorn didn't possess her astute and analytical mind. He couldn't possibly. He was male. It was up to her to solve this case—all by herself, as usual.

* * *

Praise for the first Amanda Hazard mystery,
DEAD IN THE WATER:

"Ms. Feddersen does a fine job of creating small-town life [and] readers will enjoy the colorful setting. Nick and Amanda's relationship is a fiery one, sure to keep readers coming back for more."

—*Romantic Times*

And accolades for the second Amanda mystery,
DEAD IN THE CELLAR:

"This is a mystery, romance and comedy rolled into one, and it is an excellent blend. Read this one for an evening of pure enjoyment."

—*Rendezvous*

DEAD IN THE MELON PATCH

CONNIE FEDDERSEN

ZEBRA BOOKS
KENSINGTON PUBLISHING CORP.

ZEBRA BOOKS are published by

Kensington Publishing Corp.
850 Third Avenue
New York, NY 10022

First Printing: March, 1995

Printed in the United States of America

This book is dedicated to my husband Ed and our children Christie, Jill, and Kurt, with much love.

Also, a very special thank you to husband Ed for helping me create plots and develop characters for all my books, under all my pen names, and especially for painting the artwork on the cover of this book. Ed made me his cover model for Dead In The Melon Patch. Thanks, honey. Bottoms up!

And last but hardly least, to Laurie Feigenbaum. It is both an honor and pleasure to be working with you.

One

Amanda Hazard, CPA extraordinaire, wore a look of profound concentration, as she stared down at the open book on the kitchen counter. Her well-manicured finger was poised on the first column of a time chart. Grim determination flickered in her baby blues.

Enough was enough, Amanda had decided. Country cop Nick Thorn had made one too many wisecracks about Amanda's lack of culinary skills. And the best way for her to force Thorn to eat his words was to enter her own canned green beans and peaches in the country fair. Armed with a *Kerr Home Canning Book,* a newly purchased pressure cooker, and vats of boiling green beans and syrup for peaches, Amanda was prepared to make her cooking debut.

Each year the neighboring rural communities of Vamoose and Pronto joined efforts to host a fair and carnival. This year Amanda had visions of making culinary history with blue-ribbon awards in the fruit and vegetable divisions. She would redeem herself even further by whipping up a German chocolate cake for the bake auction, from which all proceeds would be donated to purchase playground equipment for local schools.

Thorn would be very sorry indeed that he had scoffed at Amanda's lack of talent in the kitchen. She looked forward to flashing her blue ribbons in his handsome face.

Amanda smiled through the cloud of steam hovering over her stove. How hard could it be to cram a few beans into a canning jar, fill it with boiling water, then seal and stuff it in a pressure cooker? There was nothing to this cooking business, she assured herself. All she had to do was devote a little time and effort, and presto! she would become the Canning Queen of the Vamoose and Pronto Country Fair.

"Green beans," Amanda read aloud from the canning time table. "Boil five minutes, pack tightly and cook for twenty minutes at ten pounds pressure. No sweat. Even a culinary moron could do that."

With her customary efficiency, Amanda pinched a tong full of beans and rammed them in the sterilized jar. After she had added boiling water, she screwed the lid on good and tight and plunked the jar into the pressure cooker. To save time, Amanda repeated the process for the peaches and stuck them in with the beans.

She had just set the pressure cooker lid in place and turned up the heat when the phone rang. Brimming with a sense of accomplishment, Amanda strode off to answer the phone.

"Hazard's House of Fine Foods. Head cook speaking," she greeted the caller cheerily.

"Hi, doll, it's Mother," came the blaring voice from the other end of the line.

The pressure cooker hissed and sputtered in the kitchen. Amanda summoned her patience. She always needed a barrel full of it when dealing with her domineering mother.

"Hello, Mother."

"What's this nonsense about fine foods?" Mother demanded. "Everybody knows you aren't the slightest bit domestic. That's probably what ruined your first marriage, and it's most likely the reason you can't land the police chief of Podunk City."

Steam billowed and pressure increased— in the home canning cooker, too.

"That is *Vamoose*, Mother, not Podunk City." Amanda corrected through clenched teeth.

"Same difference."

Amanda put a stranglehold on the phone, envisioning Mother's neck. "I've decided to enter a cake and some canned goods in this year's fair."

"You've got to be kidding, doll!"

Amanda muttered under her breath at the condescending tone that had hounded her since childhood. "No, Mother, I'm perfectly serious about this."

"Well, if you're so determined to be domestic, I'll do the cooking for you. What do you want me to bake and can for this rinky-dink fair?"

"Nothing, Mother. That would be cheating."

"You want to win first prize, don't you?" Mother asked.

"I intend to— all by myself."

Amanda swore she heard a snicker coming down the line. So much for parental support and encouragement. But then, what did she expect?

"I'm sorry to cut you off, Mother, but I'm on a tight schedule here. The fair entries have to be at the chairperson's home for registration in an hour."

"Well then, doll, I'll make this quick."

That would be a first. Mother was as long-winded as an olympic swimmer.

Mother cleared her throat, as was her habit, and forged ahead. "I called to invite you and your cop friend to the Hazard family Labor Day picnic. Your daddy and I still haven't gotten a look at Thorn, you know. We're curious to see what your policeman is like."

Thus far, Mother hadn't had the pleasure of grilling Thorn over an open fire. The man had no idea how fortunate he was.

"I've got to run, Mother," Amanda hedged.

"You *will* be there." It was a direct order.

"We'll have to wait and see. The picnic is the same day as the fair."

"Then skip the fair. You have family obligations— like introducing us to this Thorn person."

"Good-bye, Mother. I'll be in touch."

Mother was still yackety-yakking when the weight on the pressure cooker's vent pipe clattered like a faulty car engine. Amanda dropped the receiver in its cradle and darted into the kitchen to decrease the heat.

The pressure cooker had reduced itself to a sputter and sizzle when the phone blared again. She scowled at the second interruption and stamped to the phone.

"Now what, Mother?" Amanda asked impatiently.

Obviously it wasn't Mother, for there was a long, startled pause. Mother almost never paused.

"Amanda? Is that you, sugar? This is Lula MacAdo."

"Hello, Miz MacAdo," Amanda greeted her cordially.

Everyone in Vamoose called the elderly widow *"Miz* MacAdo," out of courtesy and respect. She was the personification of what everyone's sweet, kind-hearted grandmother should look and act like— a combination of Mrs. Claus and Cinderella's Fairy Godmother. Miz MacAdo was the best cook west of the City— bar none. She had won more blue ribbons and grand championships for canned and baked goods than anyone in Vamoose County. There was nothing Miz MacAdo couldn't cook exceptionally well. Her watermelon preserves were known far and wide— which was exactly why Amanda had canned peaches and green beans. No one could compete with Miz MacAdo and hope to win first prize at the fair.

"As you know, today is the deadline for delivering entries for the canning division of the fair.

I was hoping you might be able to bring your canned goods to my house a little earlier than scheduled, sugar. I have several errands to run for the fair board before I keep my weekly hair appointment this afternoon."

Amanda craned her neck around the corner to check the pressure cooker and timer. *"How early, Miz MacAdo?"*

"Within the next half hour would be fine."

Amanda shrugged. Okay, so the beans and peaches could only cook fifteen instead of twenty minutes. No big deal. The jars could cool on the way to Miz MacAdo's farmhouse. "Sure, I'll be there as soon as I can."

Amanda could hear a muffled voice in the background.

"Good. I appreciate it."

The agitated edge to Miz MacAdo's voice caused Amanda to furrow her brow in concern. "Is everything all right out there?"

Amanda heard another whining voice and the crackling blare of the television.

"As all right as can be expected. My grand-daughter— "

Apparently Miz MacAdo had cupped her hand over the mouthpiece to toss a comment to her grumbling granddaughter. Amanda heard nothing for several seconds.

"Well, if I have to leave before you arrive," Miz MacAdo continued belatedly, "Sheila will be here watching her favorite soap opera, provided she can get the TV tuned in after last night's windstorm bent our aerial. Just bring out your fair entries and leave them at the house. I'll have them labeled, stored, and delivered with the others. And don't forget that you're invited to the Happy Homemaker Club's ice cream social this weekend."

After saying goodbye, Amanda hung up the phone and smiled to herself. Miz MacAdo was a woman after her own heart. Lula was organized to a fault. Efficient to a flaw. Even at age seventy-two, Lula MacAdo set a rigorous pace that would wear out folks half her age. She was a Pink Lady volunteer at the county hospital, served on the fair board and church board. She baked pies, cakes, and cookies for every community fundraiser and she still had time to wait— hand and foot— on her lazy granddaughter.

Amanda had yet to get the full scoop on the slothful Sheila, despite their having met once or twice. However, in Amanda's opinion— and she was never without one on any subject— Sheila MacAdo was the exact opposite of her ambitious grandmother. To Sheila, *work* appeared to be a four-letter word. She avoided it at all cost.

Casting the thought aside, Amanda hurriedly filled the sink and plunged the steaming pressure cooker into the cold water. Metal crackled and the cooker hissed like a leaky radiator hose. Amanda figured the quick-cool method would reduce the steam and save time.

While the pressure cooker cooled, Amanda padded across the antiquated linoleum floor to retrieve her socks and Justin Roper boots. By the time she returned to the kitchen she could safely remove the lid from the cooker without the risk of being scalded by steam.

The liquid in the canning jars was still bubbling like crazy, so Amanda fanned them with a tea towel. Even if the beans and peaches hadn't cooked the full twenty minutes they looked good enough to win blue ribbons, Amanda assured herself. Nick Thorn was going to be very impressed.

With visions of blue ribbons dancing in her head, Amanda loaded the hot jars in an extra large shoe box and whizzed out the front door of her rented farm home.

She would have plenty of time to reach Miz MacAdo's house— with minutes to burn.

Amanda swore inventively when she cranked the Toyota's engine to note the fuel gauge was sitting on empty. She would have to detour into Vamoose for a pit stop at Thatcher's Oil and Gas.

Amanda stepped on the accelerator and sped off, throwing aside gravel and dust. If she ran out of gas she could coast into town, provided she had enough momentum and a strong tailwind.

The things she did to impress Thorn. Ah well, it was all over Vamoose that she and Thorn were an item. Velma, the beautician, had sent the news down her grapevine and carried it to Last Chance Cafe on her lunch break. Thorn was

pleased, of course. It was one of those male pos-
session things.

Singing along with Oklahoma-grown Garth
Brooks on the country radio station, Amanda
zoomed into town on gas fumes and a prayer.
She coasted the last hundred yards after her red
Toyota guzzled its last drop of fuel. When, she
wondered, were the automotive geniuses of the
world going to design and perfect solar-powered
vehicles? None too soon to satisfy her!

Amanda exhaled an impatient breath and
glanced at her watch. Her pit stop at Thatcher's
Oil and Gas had taken longer than planned.
Thaddeus Thatcher had cornered her, feeding
her trivia about the brands and durability of tires
under various road conditions. He had gone into
extensive detail, particularly in explaining the
reason her tires had worn so thin. Thaddeus had
strongly suggested— given Amanda's wheeltramp
and wheelbase— that she order a new set of tires
before she had a blowout. Because of Thaddeus's
lengthy conversation, Amanda was running late.

Glancing around to ensure Deputy Sykes
wasn't parked beside Whatsit River to stop
speeding motorists, Amanda put the pedal to
the metal and sailed over the bridge to make up
for lost time. She veered around the corner onto
the gravel road leading to Lula MacAdo's farm
home.

The wind damage from the previous night's

summer thunderstorm was more noticeable south of Vamoose. Amanda had only gotten a few sprinkles and wind gusts at her farm home. Farther south, she could see plastic grocery sacks and cardboard boxes clinging to barbwire fences. A few tree limbs had snapped, hanging at odd angles like broken arms.

The brief rain shower hadn't even settled the dust on Commissioner Brown's ungraded country roads, leaving washboarded intersections for Amanda's lightweight foreign car to bounce over. Furthermore, the Johnsongrass, sunflowers, and cottonwood striplings in the bar ditches were taller than a giraffe's belly. One of these days, Amanda decided, she was going to call Commissioner Brown and bend his ear about the negligence to the county roads. It was one of her pet peeves.

When Amanda wheeled inside the white picket fence that surrounded MacAdo Farm, she grumbled to herself. Lula's fifteen-year-old Ford LTD wasn't in the driveway. It looked as though Amanda would be stuck with Sheila.

Clamping the shoebox containing her future blue-ribbon, prizewinning beans and peaches under one arm, Amanda strode onto the porch and rang the door bell. There was no response from the slothful Sheila.

"Sheila! It's Amanda Hazard," she yelled at the closed door.

Nothing, but silence.

Grumbling, Amanda opened the door and

poked her head inside to see crackling waves of static flitting across the television screen like a blizzard. A cup of coffee was sitting on the end table beside the leather recliner, but there was no Sheila.

Lining the mantel of the fireplace was a carefully organized display of trophies and blue ribbons. A recently dusted bookshelf, filled with references on cooking, canning, and gardening sat in the far corner of the room. Each book was arranged alphabetically by title.

That was Lula through and through, Amanda reminded herself. "Organized" was Lula Mac-Ado's middle name.

Announcing herself once again, Amanda turned toward the kitchen. The caterwauling of Lula's tabby cat drew Amanda's attention. The chubby tomcat was perched on the window sill beside jars of green beans, cherries, peaches, and watermelon preserves. Four stylish cotton dresses, fashioned by the best seamstresses of Vamoose's Happy Homemaker Club, hung over the door casing in plastic bags— numbered, labeled and ready to be entered in the sewing competition at the fair.

Amanda strode over to inspect the other jar of beans and frowned. Perfectly proportioned green beans stood on their snapped ends, carefully wedged together and neatly packed. Amanda scoffed at the absurdity of spending valuable time lining a canning jar with such precision. She could understand why pickles might

be lined up in a jar, but certainly not beans.
Who the heck was going to reach into a jar and
nibble on a green bean?

Amanda had cut *her* beans into bite-size pieces
and crammed them up to the neck of the jar.
And now she was certain she would win the bean
category— hands down. The judges would laugh
themselves silly when they saw the way the other
entrant had arranged her vegetables.

The jar of peaches was just as impractically
packaged, Amanda noted with a smirk. The
fruit was stacked in clear-colored syrup rather
than the peachy-yellow juice of Amanda's prizewinning entry. Winning blue ribbons would be
a snap, Amanda confidently assured herself.

When the oversized cat glanced up and
yowled, Amanda moved to stroke its broad head.
But before she could touch him, the cat
bounded out the open window. Amanda craned
her neck to see the tomcat hop onto the broken
picket fence . . .

And then she saw it— or rather *her.* From the
window, she could see a sandy blond head and
bare legs visible among the vines. Quickly setting her jars aside, Amanda dashed out the
kitchen door to the covered porch to assess the
situation. Sure enough, there was a motionless
body sprawled facedown in Lula's watermelon
patch.

Amanda let herself through the gate only to
see Sheila's head bookended by a melon that
had split in half, oozing juice into the victim's

sandy blond hair. Amanda stepped over the melons and tangling vines to check for a pulse in Sheila's neck.

There was none. Sheila MacAdo was missing her favorite soap opera— one final time.

Two

Standing up to look around, Amanda took a good look at the wooden ladder that had collided with the broken fence. At first glance, it appeared that Sheila had climbed the ladder and had taken the fatal fall. Amanda could see wasps buzzing around the hive just beneath the eave of the house. She glanced back to see if Sheila had been stung. There were no red welts on Sheila's long legs, well-displayed in skin-tight Daisy Duke short-shorts.

Amanda stared up at the roof, noting the broken antenna. That was obviously the reason Sheila had not gotten good reception for her soap opera, Amanda concluded. The windstorm had played havoc with the aerial.

Cat prints in the freshly tilled dirt indicated the tabby had already appraised the situation before Amanda arrived. To the average observer, Sheila's fall from the ladder— across the picket fence and into the melon patch— might have looked to be a stroke of bad luck. But Amanda Hazard's finely tuned instincts suggested something more when she noticed the garden rake propped against the fence. She glanced back at the freshly tilled soil.

Had someone given Sheila a shove and then raked away incriminating footprints once they were certain the victim was dead?

Obviously, thought Amanda.

She knew for a fact that Lula MacAdo was a stickler for organization— same as Amanda. That was one of the reasons Amanda regarded Lula as her kindred spirit. If Lula had used the garden rake, it would have been returned to its proper place.

Knowing what Amanda knew about Sheila, the woman was as lazy as they came. She would never be caught dead raking the garden— only caught dead *lying* in it.

With suspicions buzzing around her head like wasps, Amanda wheeled around to inspect the tool shed. As expected, Lula's gardening tools were hanging in alphabetical order on the wall— hoe, hose, and shovel. The hook where the rake belonged was empty. Whoever had caused Sheila's fall into the melons had forgotten to restore the rake to its hook after covering the incriminating tracks.

It was foul play, Amanda concluded, that caused Sheila MacAdo to crack her melon, and probably her neck, too.

It was time to call in Vamoose's sexy country cop and open an investigation. The slothful Sheila MacAdo was in for a long, uninterrupted rest, but Amanda had every intention of sniffing out the culprit who had put Sheila to sleep—permanently.

In grim resignation, Amanda scurried from the garden toward her Toyota. It would take thirty minutes to drive out to the farm where Nick Thorn was out working the field in preparation for fall wheat planting. Thorn was renting the land Amanda had inherited from Elmer Jolly.

Amanda had no intention of reporting this incident to Deputy Sykes, even if he was on duty. The man was nowhere near Thorn's caliber when it came to law enforcement. The rookie's first reaction was to panic and repeat every word spoken to him.

Shoving the gear into reverse, Amanda wheeled around and then burned rubber. She hoped that Thorn could investigate and remove the body before Lula MacAdo returned from her errands. Seeing her granddaughter sprawled in the garden was a shock the elderly widow didn't need.

The Toyota shot off like a rocket, bouncing over the washboarded roads. When a *boom* resounded beneath her, Amanda clamped a tight grip on the wheel to prevent the car from fishtailing and nosediving into the ditch as she slowly came to a stop. The *thump* beneath the driver's side of the car indicated Thaddeus Thatcher's prediction had come true. Amanda had blown a tire. Damn, what lousy timing.

Slamming the door behind her, Amanda stared at the exposed rim of the tire. She glanced down the road, trying to decide what to do. It was entirely too hot to jog back to the house or hike to town. Her shoulders slumped in relief when she saw a gray pickup truck approaching.

When the old clunker ground to a halt beside her, Amanda pasted on a smile. Bubba Hix, dressed in his gray service station uniform, sat behind the wheel of the truck. Bubba Jr. stood on the seat beside his father, wearing nothing but a cloth diaper and sucking his dirty thumb. Sis Hix, with her stringy brown hair tucked beneath a cap that read Bad Hair Day, was propped against the passenger door. The overweight couple and their eighteen-month-old son glanced at her curiously. The odor hovering around the cab of the truck made Amanda's eyes water. The word *ripe* instantly sprang to mind.

"Want me to change your tire for you, 'Manda?" Bubba generously offered.

Ordinarily, her answer would have been yes. Today it was no. Amanda had to track down Officer Thorn— pronto.

"I would really appreciate it if you could give me a ride out to the old Jolly farm," Amanda requested. Without giving Bubba time to refuse, she opened the creaking pickup door and waited for Sis to slide over on the seat. "I know it's out of your way, but I need to speak with Thorn immediately. It's a bit of an emergency."

Bubba glanced down at the watch on his hairy arm. "I reckon I've got time before I have to report back to work at the filling station. Hop in, 'Manda."

"If Thaddeus complains, tell him I'll explain later," Amanda insisted.

When Sis slid over to grant her room, Amanda sank onto the seat. The odor of sweat and greasy hair permeated the cab of the old truck. She willfully ignored it until Bubba Jr. toddled over his mother's legs and planted himself on Amanda's lap. A dried milk mustache was caked on Bubba Jr.'s upper lip. There was enough dirt lodged under the boy's fingernails to fill a flower pot. Amanda endured as best she could while Bubba Jr. chattered nonstop in a language only his parents seemed to understand.

"Did you get much rain last night?" Sis questioned as she picked her teeth with her fingernail.

"Just a sprinkle."

"We had nothing but wind," Bubba put in as he shifted gears and roared off with the sound of a bad muffler trailing behind them. "I thought the wind was gonna blow our trailer house plumb over. It kept Bubba Jr. awake half the night."

When Bubba Jr. began to jabber again to Amanda, she glanced at Sis for translation.

"He said: Guess what?"

Amanda offered the dirty-faced kid a smile. "What, Bubba Jr.?"

The toddler yammered excitedly in unintelligible sentences.

"He said we're gonna have another baby,"

Bubba proudly announced. "We just got the good news from Doctor Simms awhile ago."

The Hixes were populating Vamoose again? No doubt Sis Junior would make a fine addition to the family. "Congratulations."

"If it's a girl, we'll call her Sissy," Sis proclaimed.

Somehow, Amanda figured she would say something like that.

"Make a left at the next mile line," Amanda instructed. "Thorn is working ground west of the old Jolly homestead."

Bubba glanced at his watch and gunned the old jalopy. As it bounced over the rough road, Amanda inwardly groaned. Unless she was mistaken— and she was sure she wasn't since she rarely ever was— Bubba Jr. had just wet his diaper while sitting in her lap. Her Rocky Mountain jeans would never be the same.

The instant the truck rolled to a stop, Amanda shoved open the door and stepped out, frowning at the damp spot on her jeans. "Thanks for the lift."

"That's what neighbors are for." Bubba waved a thick arm and shot off with his rusted tailpipe blowing black smoke.

Amanda stared at the orange Allis-Chalmers tractor that was kicking up dust on the far side of the field. Thorn's black 4x4 truck, with the hay fork protruding from its bed, was sitting on the slope of the ditch.

Amanda started toward the truck. She needed

to talk to Thorn— now. She didn't have time to wait for him to work his way toward her. Sheila MacAdo was sprawled in the melon patch, growing riper by the minute in the blazing summer sun.

Nick Thorn scowled when he saw his 4x4 truck bouncing across the freshly worked ground. It had to be Hazard, he deduced. No self-respecting farmer would leave tracks across a field.

When the black truck came to a halt directly in the tractor's path, Nick muttered a curse and pulled down on the throttle. He stepped down to meet a hot blast of summer wind and Hazard's shapely figure wrapped in jeans and a cotton knit blouse.

This blue-eyed and blond CPA always looked good, no matter what she was wearing, Nick noted. It gave him a pleasing sense of possessive male pride knowing she was his woman. The only problem was that, with Nick's hectic schedule of farming and policing the countryside, he had little time for pleasurable pursuits. As for Hazard, she was usually up to her gorgeous neck in tax files. After solving two crimes, her fame and popularity had escalated to the point where she proudly claimed to have the entire population of Vamoose as her clients— save one. Nick still hadn't turned his tax forms over to her. The time wasn't quite right for that.

"Thorn, I need you *now*," Amanda insisted.

Nick waggled his black brows and started to unbutton his shirt.

"Not that kind of need . . ." Amanda's gaze dipped to the dark matting of hair on his muscled chest and reminded herself this wasn't the time or place. "Tonight, Thorn. Your place."

He beamed with anticipation. It had been a long dry spell—like the weather conditions in Vamoose.

"We have a problem," Amanda began.

"We do? I thought our relationship was progressing rather smoothly these days."

Amanda gave her head a grim shake. "I wasn't talking about *us*, Thorn. I've found another dead body."

Nick groaned aloud. Hazard had that look in her baby blues. "Another prospective murder victim, I suppose."

Amanda gritted her teeth. She should be accustomed to Thorn's skepticism by now, but she wasn't. Just once she wished he would take her seriously and leap into an investigation with both booted feet, rather than dragging them.

"I drove out to Miz MacAdo's to deliver my green beans and peaches—"

Thorn's brows jackknifed. "What the hell are you talking about?"

"I canned fruit and veggies for the country fair and—"

She was interrupted by a burst of laughter that drowned out the tractor's idling engine.

"Give me a break, Hazard. You're helpless

without a microwave, so there's no way you can compete in an old-fashioned country fair."

This was precisely why Amanda had entered her canned food. She was going to shove her prizewinning beans and peaches down his throat.

"The point is that I arrived at the farm after Lula left to run errands in town. I found Sheila dead in the garden. Somebody had cracked her melon."

"You should have contacted Benny Sykes," Nick insisted. "I happen to be on vacation and I need to get this ground worked ASAP. And thank you so much for leaving tracks on my seed bed. You cost me an extra two hours of work."

"To hell with your seed bed!" she blared at him. "We have a murder to solve. And you know perfectly well that Deputy Sykes is only good at rattling off police jargon and handing out speeding tickets."

Nick exhaled a long-suffering sigh, pivoted around, and climbed inside the tractor cab to turn off the fuel and ignition switches. He may as well nip Hazard's suspicions in the bud so he could get back to work. She would make his life miserable until he did.

"Scoot over," Nick demanded when Hazard sat down on the driver's side of his truck. "I'm driving."

Amanda glanced down at the worked ground and then stared at the chisel that was hooked behind the tractor. "Why aren't you plowing like everybody else around Vamoose and Pronto?"

Now what? The woman inherited a few hundred acres of land from a deceased client and she suddenly thought she was an expert farmer. Nick would never have rented the property from Hazard if he had suspected she would turn into the landlady from hell. Why couldn't she stick to her accounting and let him manage her farm land?

"Unlike the older generation of farmers who are entrenched in tradition, I'm not sold on plowing," Nick explained. "We haven't had much rain and the ground is already as hard as concrete. I don't want to pull up chunks the size of boulders. If we don't get rain, I won't be able to get a decent seed bed to plant wheat. Besides that, my cow peas are about to wilt. It has been a hard year for farm crops."

"But since I'm your landlady, shouldn't *I* have a say in what you do with *my* land? Ab Hendershot said—"

"Forget what Hendershot said. I'm renting this property and you'll get your payment, no matter how good or bad the wheat crop turns out to be."

Amanda let the subject drop. Thorn was always out of sorts after spending endless hours in solitary confinement on his tractor. She reminded herself that he didn't enjoy having her tell him what to do any more than she enjoyed being bossed around. Anyway, Vamoose's most recent murder took precedence over Thorn's field work. She would have his cooperation, even if she had to drag it out of him!

"I have a theory about Sheila's death." Amanda grabbed the armrest to brace herself as the truck bounced over the terrace ridge at an excessive speed.

"Now, Hazard," Nick patronized. "Don't try to influence my thinking before I have a chance to assess the scene of the accident— "

"Murder," she quickly corrected. "It's my belief that Sheila didn't wind up dead all by herself."

Nick rolled his eyes and stepped harder on the accelerator. The sooner he reached the MacAdo residence the sooner he could file his report and get back to work.

When Nick passed Hazard's Toyota on the side of the road he glanced questioningly at her.

"Blowout," she informed him. "I hitched a ride with Bubba and Sis Hix. Bubba Jr. had an accident in my lap, in case you're being polite enough not to ask what that unpleasant smell is."

Nick wheeled into the driveway and stepped out into the summer heat. Damn, he wished it would rain and cool things down. It would also give him an excuse to take a few days off. He was going stir-crazy driving around in his tractor, getting nowhere. Hell, he could have toured the whole continental United States in the time he had spent driving his tractor in monotonous circles.

Amanda motioned Thorn toward the garden at the back of the house. "There." She directed his attention to the thirty-something Sheila who was exactly where Amanda had left her forty-five minutes earlier.

Upon closer inspection, Nick discovered Hazard's assessment of Sheila's physical condition was correct. Sheila was the only one of the three of them who wasn't sweating.

Nick surveyed the broken picket fence and the ladder that had crashed into it. The drone of insects drew his attention to the wasp nest beneath the eave.

"I know what you're thinking, Thorn," Amanda said, following his contemplative gaze. "But I checked for wasp stings, without touching the body, of course. I didn't see any welts."

Nick unfolded himself from the ground and stepped back to appraise the broken aerial on the roof. "Sheila must have been trying to make repairs— "

"So she wouldn't have to miss her favorite soap," Amanda finished impatiently. "Her reason for being on the ladder is not as important as why she was pushed off of it. Do you have any idea who might want to have Sheila conveniently out of the way?"

"Her grandmother?" Nick ventured sarcastically. "Sheila moved back in with Lula after her third marriage broke up. Maybe Lula was fed up with her lazy granddaughter."

"Her third marriage?" Amanda glanced at the body in the melon patch. "Exactly how old was Sheila?"

"Thirty-two," Nick reported. "She was a couple of years behind me in high school. 'Fast and easy Sheila,' we called her.''

"And I suppose *you* called her a few times yourself," Amanda added accusingly.

Nick shifted awkwardly from one foot to the other and focused on the wasp nest. "Ancient history, Hazard. I figured Sheila was trying to make up for the lack of affection she received from her parents. When her folks split up, they dumped her on Lula's doorstep. Lula tried to control Sheila but she was a handful— and then some."

He gestured toward Sheila's skimpy attire. "Sheila dressed to attract male attention for as long as I can remember. She got plenty of it, but it was never enough to satisfy her. She was into stealing boyfriends and husbands for the sport of it. As you can imagine, most of her friends were men, not women."

"A regular *femme fatale* who probably harbored enough sordid secrets that somebody wanted to keep Pandora's box shut— permanently," Amanda speculated.

Nick expelled a snort and headed for the house. "Come on, Hazard, don't start with that cause, motive, and suspect business. It's clear that Sheila took an accidental spill. You're trying to make something of nothing, probably because I'm on the first vacation I've had in two years and I have acres of ground to work before I return to patrol duty."

"There you go with your unprofessional attitude again," she muttered, following him into the house. "And don't give me that 'I've got no time to be bothered with your nonsense' look, either, Thorn."

Inside, Nick snatched up the phone and dialed the medical examiner. "I've got a stiff here for you to examine." He gave quick, precise directions to the farm and hung up.

When Nick strode off, Amanda stared at him in amazement. "Where are you going? You can't leave the scene of the crime."

"You obviously did."

"Only to track you down," she qualified. "That doesn't count."

Nick paused on the porch and stared into the distance. "After I change your tire you can run along home while I take care of this matter."

"But I have suspicions—"

"Or better yet," Nick strategically interrupted, "you can drive the Allis while I wrap this up. I've ridden her long and hard for a week."

Amanda glared at him. "Don't be crude, Thorn. And anyway, I don't know diddlysquat about driving your Allis tractor."

"It's time you learned," Nick declared as he ushered Amanda toward his pickup. "Put the Allis in third gear and leave the chisel in the ground at the same depth as it is now. And don't mess with the other levers in the cab. I'll be out to relieve you when I'm finished here."

"Damn it, Thorn. We have a murder to solve," Amanda growled as he pushed her into his pickup truck.

Nick climbed into the other seat. With one hand braced on the steering wheel and the other clamped around the key in the ignition he stared long and hard at Hazard. "Okay, let's get this over with. What has brought you to the wild conclusion that Sheila didn't accidentally fall off her ladder and land *kersplat* in the melon patch?"

Amanda lifted her chin to meet Thorn's mocking gaze. "Because the murderer left the rake in the garden."

"The *rake*," Nick repeated as he cranked the engine.

"Whoever shoved Sheila took time to rake over the incriminating footprints in the dirt and didn't replace the tool in Lula MacAdo's shed."

Nick groaned as he shifted gears. "Hell's bells, Hazard, how do you come up with this stuff? Being city born and bred, you probably aren't familiar with our countrified expressions. But here's one you should know and remember: Shit happens."

Amanda gnashed her teeth and tried to remind herself that Thorn did not possess her astute and analytical mind. He couldn't possibly. He was male. It was up to her to solve this case—all by herself, as usual.

"I am only being logical, Thorn. Lula MacAdo is as much a stickler for organizational details as I am. Everything has its place in her world, and those things *stay* in their place. Lula's tax records are proof positive that she likes things neat and tidy. You have never seen such precision until you've seen Lula's expenses and investments for her income tax files. And one look around her home indicates her penchant for precise organization in her personal life as well. The only things out of place in that house belong to Sheila. Lula's granddaughter was obviously a lazy slob."

Nick pulled up behind the Toyota and thrust out his hand, silently requesting the key. While he retrieved the spare tire from the trunk and jacked up the car, Amanda positioned herself behind him, wondering if a kick in the butt would provoke Thorn to take her suspicions seriously. Probably not. Thorn had gotten in the habit of doubting Amanda's hunches. Another one of those male things, she diagnosed. Men did not like to admit women were right, unless they were left with no other alternative.

"Now let me make sure I've got this straight, Hazard. You have concluded that Sheila was intentionally pushed off the ladder because the rake was in the garden instead of the shed."

"Right," she said with absolute certainty.

"And who are your suspects?" Nick half-heartedly indulged her.

"You would know better than I would, having lived around Vamoose most of your life. How many men was the divorcee seeing who might have reason to feel threatened by her?"

Nick loosened the lugs and tossed the remnants of the ruined tire aside. "Counting her ex-husbands?"

"Yes. I shouldn't have to remind you that jealous rage is a common motive for murder. Heck, the newspapers are rife with such gory stories. I swear the media feeds on that stuff like a pack of starving wolves. In my opinion . . ."

Nick replaced the tire and listened to Hazard spout another of her opinions about the media and their aggravating habit of sensationalism. It was one of her many pet peeves, as he recalled.

When the Toyota was fit for travel, Nick handed Amanda the keys. "You have four hours of fuel left in the tractor. I should be back before then. If not, leave the Allis by the field gate. We'll do supper at my place tonight and I'll fill you in on the details after I speak with the coroner."

When Thorn thrust Amanda into her compact car, she grumbled at him. "I can see that I'm going to have to investigate all by myself."

"Now, Hazard— "

"It was no accident, Thorn," Amanda insisted. "I have a feeling things look much simpler than they really are. You should dust the place for fingerprints."

Nick's midnight-black eyes bulged in disbelief. "You want me to *dust* the *garden*? No way, Hazard, your weird suspicions have led you astray on this particular case," he assured her. "Sheila obviously climbed the ladder to repair the antenna so she could watch her favorite soap opera. She was startled by the wasps under the eave, and maybe even stung. I won't know that for sure until the medical examiner arrives. When Sheila fell, she landed on the picket fence and then fell into the melons. End of story.

"Just because Sheila ran fast and loose since junior high school doesn't mean her ex-husbands or her present boyfriends were out to get her. And one lousy rake propped against the garden fence is not sufficient grounds for an all-out investigation. Now go work the field you inherited from Elmer Jolly."

"Thorn, don't talk down to me."

"I have no choice," he said, as he braced his brawny arms against the top of her compact car and stared down at her through the open window.

"Don't try to be cute, Thorn. That wasn't what I meant. I get talked down to enough by Mother, every blasted time she calls."

"How is Mother, by the way?"

"She is her usual domineering self. She invited you to the Hazard Labor Day celebration so she could meet you in person and decide if you're good enough for me."

"Am I?"

He flashed her one of his smiles that could buckle Amanda's knees if she hadn't been sitting down. But she refused to be mesmerized by a man who oozed masculine sensuality.

"No, Thorn, you are not the man for me if you refuse to take my hunches and suspicions seriously. You can attend the get-together without me. I'll probably be too busy searching for clues in this case that you insist don't exist."

"And I suppose our long-awaited rendezvous at my place is off for the night, too," he muttered sourly.

"You got that right, Thorn."

When Hazard sped off, Nick stomped over to grab the ruined tire and then tossed it in the back of his truck. He and that voluptuous blonde got along fine until dead bodies turned up in Vamoose. And then *wham*. Hazard cried murder and nagged him to death to investigate.

True, the accountant-turned-sleuth had been right twice before. But this case was entirely different. Nick would, of course, follow proper police procedure and ask Lula MacAdo a few questions. But he was not going to accuse every Tom, Dick, and Harry who had fooled around with Sheila of foul play.

Nick had twice as much farm ground to work now that he was renting Amanda's land. There was fencing to repair, cattle to move to greener pastures, and land to till. He didn't have time for Hazard's goose chases. But in her estimation, no one died of natural causes around Vamoose. Each body was a potential investigation for that hacksaw detective who was sure she had missed her true calling in life.

"All because of a damned rake," Nick scowled as he drove back to the MacAdo farm. If he keeled over in the driveway from heat exhaustion and bit the dust, Hazard would probably open an investigation. It was so like her to be suspicious.

Dreading another night alone, Nick propped himself against the side of his truck and waited for the medical examiner to confirm what he believed to be true. Sheila MacAdo had been stung— or at least frightened by the wasps— and had fallen into the fence.

This time Hazard was way off base, Nick convinced himself. But of course, she would wear out those gorgeous legs of hers hitting the pavement to scare up facts before she arrived at the inevitable conclusion for herself.

You simply could not tell that woman anything!

CRIME OF THE MEDIC PATCH 41

Amanda smiled in satisfaction. She had won the
first skirmish.

Three

Amanda parked her car on the edge of the
road noticing that the Johnsongrass and sunflowers all but concealed her vehicle from view.
She hiked off across the field, nearly twisting
her ankle on the uneven terrain.

After climbing into the tractor cab, Amanda
stared in frustration at the various levers and
gauges. She silently fumed, knowing Thorn had
sent her to the boondocks to work the field so she
would be out of his hair. He and the medical examiner were probably having a good laugh about
her suspicions at this very moment. The jerks.

Exasperated, Amanda switched on the ignition. Nothing happened. She studied the knobs
and gauges on the dashboard and then glanced
up at the radio and air conditioner that sat above
the front window of the cab. Okay, so what is
the trick to starting this confounded machine?

Carefully she examined each knob and gauge.
Grabbing the black knob that read: Fuel Injection, Amanda gave it a tug and then tried the
ignition. The Allis-Chalmers roared to life.

Amanda smiled in satisfaction. She had won the first skirmish.

After a series of trial-and-error maneuvers, Amanda revved the engine up to enough horsepower to pull the implement attached behind the tractor. She took her foot off the clutch and the tractor lurched like a bucking bronc, bouncing over the rough terrain. Amanda gritted her teeth, fearing they'd shake loose. She negotiated her first corner, noting she had skipped a wide space before getting back on track.

Thorn's corners had been smooth and evenly turned. Amanda's were not. No doubt, this was to be a subtle reminder that she was out of her element— in the wheat field and in the investigative field. Amanda did not agree. She smelled a rat at MacAdo Farm . . .

The crackle of the CB radio drew her attention. She fiddled with the squelch and turned up the volume. To her surprise, other farmers working in nearby fields had gotten wind of Thorn's and the medical examiner's arrival at the MacAdo house. Speculations were running rampant.

"Ab?" Clive Barnstall's gravelly voice came over the CB, loud and clear. "Can you see what's going on at the MacAdo place?"

The CB shrilled and Amanda pricked her ears to eavesdrop on Ab Hendershot's reply.

"Looks like Nick Thorn is hauling a body out of the garden," Ab replied.

"Can you tell who it is?" This from Harry Ogelbee, Amanda deduced. She had become well-acquainted with all three men during her last unofficial investigation. For a time they had been possible suspects.

"I'll be damned," Ab crowed. "It looks like Sheila. Lula sure as hell never wore shorts *that* short!"

"I bet there's a lot of men around Vamoose and Pronto who'll be breathing easier now that Sheila has two-stepped into that Great Honky-Tonk in the Sky," Clive inserted.

Alarm bells went off in Amanda's head. Whether Clive knew it or not, he was suggesting a motive that could have provoked this disaster. She silently smirked at Thorn's attempt to isolate her for the duration of his open-and-shut investigation. More than likely, Amanda was going to get an earful of clues while riding in circles around this field.

"Sheila's first husband, Alvin Priddle, was grumbling about her while he was here yesterday repairing the hydraulics on my tractor," Harry Ogelbee put in.

Amanda rammed her hand into her purse to grab a note pad. When she opened her investigation, she would be armed and ready with possible suspects and motives.

Unfortunately, in her haste to retrieve pen and paper, her elbow smacked into the levers beside her. To her dismay, she knocked the three-point takeoff and hydraulic lift forward. The chisel she was pulling dug its metal claws into the ground, causing the tractor to groan, lurch, and strain like an overworked plow horse. When she tried to undo the damage, she accidentally pushed one of the other levers in the wrong direction and the hinged machinery attached to the tractor flipped up and folded itself in thirds.

Damnation, this was all Thorn's fault, she scowled. The tractor looked like a giant duck with folded wings scudding along the ground. Every time Amanda tried to shove one or the other of the levers forward, the tractor bucked and snorted and the implement flapped.

"Who's over there working the ground Thorn rented?" Harry Ogelbee questioned.

"Don't know."

"Well, that clown doesn't know what the hell he's doing. Thorn is gonna be spittin' mad if that incompetent kid tears up his tractor and equipment."

No kidding! Amanda thought as she stamped on the clutch to bring the tractor to a halt. One at a time, she experimented with the levers. Finally, the floating arms of the chisel dropped back to the ground. After several minutes of tampering with the knobs and hydraulic levers that Thorn told her not to touch, Amanda managed to dig the implement into the ground where it belonged. Mission accomplished, she eased out on the clutch and rumbled forward.

"I saw Sheila's third husband at Last Chance Cafe this morning," Ab started up again. "Royce Shirley didn't have any kind words for his ex-wife.

According to Royce, Sheila was suing the pants off him, even though she was the one running around on him before they split the sheets."

Amanda could identify with Royce's frustration. Her ex-husband— curse him wherever he was— had pulled the same stunt on her. Amanda frowned, wondering why the farmers hadn't mentioned Husband Number Two. Wasn't he the vindictive type?

"One thing is for sure," Clive inserted, "there'll be a lot less traffic down these country roads now that Sheila bought the farm."

"Yeah, like Hugh Wilmer's," Harry chuckled. "Just because he farmed part of the MacAdo ground, he probably thought none of us knew why he made so many stops at the house. He was paying rent in more ways than one."

Amanda jotted down the names and made a mental note to call for an appointment at Velma Hertzog's Beauty Boutique. The resident beautician could supply tidbits of information about Sheila's history, as well as the scuttlebutt surrounding the divorcee.

"I guess Doralee Muchmore won't be spilling any tears over her cousin, either," Ab commented. "She and Sheila never did get along. As I recall, the two of them got into a catfight in high school and were both expelled."

"That was when Sheila stole Doralee's boyfriend and never gave him back, wasn't it?" Clive asked.

"Sure 'nuff," Ab came back. "Shortly after

that, Sheila got herself engaged to Alvin Priddle. I bet Sheila and Doralee haven't spoken a civil word to each other since."

Amanda made note of the fact that Doralee had been head over heels for Sheila's first husband. It sounded as if a long-harbored grudge might have been at work. The old love triangle was the motive of many a murder. Amanda had learned that much from watching reruns of *Magnum P.I.* and *Perry Mason.*

"The ambulance just pulled out," Ab reported over the CB.

"I think I saw Lula's Ford LTD coming down the road," Clive observed. "Looks like Nick Thorn is going to have to break the bad news to Lula. Don't envy him that. As much trouble as Sheila was to the men of the world, she was all Lula had left."

Amanda yelped and dropped her note pad when the tractor plunged down the steep slope of the terrace. The steering wheel spun furiously and machinery clattered behind her. Amanda had been so busy taking notes that she had strayed off course to chisel ground that had already been worked. The machinery behind the tractor clanked and whined as Amanda tried to turn a sharp corner. Thorn was going to give her hell when he saw what a mess she had made of his carefully worked field.

Well tough, thought Amanda. She never claimed to be a wizard with tractors and machinery.

"I can't imagine who's working Thorn's ground," Harry piped up. "The Allis is swerving all over the place. It sure as hell must be some dumb-ass kid. I hope Thorn isn't paying that idiot good wages, because he won't be getting his money's worth."

Amanda slumped lower in the seat when she saw the monster John Deere tractor on the far side of the fence.

"Clive, can you see what model of car is sitting by Thorn's gate? I'd sure like to know who that fool over there is so I don't make the mistake of hiring him."

"Nope. The weed's are too tall. I can't see a damned thing."

Thank you, Commissioner Brown. You saved me from humiliating embarrassment.

"The Allis is weaving all over the field and you should see these corners!" Clive added with a chuckle. "It will take Thorn four diagonal trips across the field to clean up the mess that kid is making."

"I can see them," Ab came back. "Thorn is going to be fit to be tied. That knothead also dug a rut in the terrace ridge that'll have to be repaired."

Amanda scowled at the insults. She was going to charge all three man extra for computing their income taxes after all the wisecracks they had made about her tractor-driving skills— or rather, the lack thereof.

When the farmers turned their conversations

to grumblings about dry weather conditions, the astronomical cost of fuel, and fertilizer and the low price of wheat, Amanda switched off the CB and contemplated what she had learned. She had gleaned the names of four possible suspects by eavesdropping.

Doralee Muchmore held a grudge against Sheila for stealing and marrying her high school sweetheart. Said high school sweetheart, Alvin Priddle, had never forgiven Sheila for walking out on him. Husband Number Three, Royce Shirley, had been heard cursing his ex-wife at the cafe. Hugh Wilmer was known to be making frequent stops at MacAdo Farm, under the pretense of visiting with his landladies.

Amanda wondered what happened to Husband Number Two and what Hugh Wilmer's married status was. He could have irritated Sheila and she might have threatened to tattle to Hugh's wife— provided he had one. Amanda could have been digging up all sorts of interesting facts around Vamoose and Pronto if she hadn't been stuck out in the middle of nowhere on this tractor, botching up Thorn's field and drawing smirks from neighboring farmers.

Despite Thorn's attempt to shuttle her out of the way, Amanda vowed to investigate the circumstances surrounding Sheila MacAdo's fatal fall into the melon patch. Lula MacAdo was one of Amanda's favorite clients. If foul play had been involved— and Amanda was sure it had— truth and justice would prevail!

* * *

"What in the hell have you been doing to my field!" Nick howled when Amanda stepped down from the cab of the tractor.

"Don't start with me, Thorn," Amanda warned him. "I did the best I could, considering you gave me no instructions, other than to drive in third gear. And furthermore, this happens to be *my* field. You're only a tenant, as you may recall."

Nick surveyed the skips in the corners where weeds were waving their green heads in the wind. The upper terrace had a ditch that would have to be repaired, costing him extra hours of work. This was turning out to be an exceptionally bad day.

"Well? What did the medical examiner have to say?"

"Sheila had a broken neck and a chest wound where the point of the picket fence stabbed her," Nick grimly reported. "There was no evidence of struggle."

"Of course not. One hard shove on the ladder would have done the trick."

Thorn's massive shoulders dropped as he expelled an exasperated breath. "Damn it to hell, Hazard, it was an accident, pure and simple. I questioned Lula when she came home. She told me Sheila was grumbling about the poor TV reception. Lula finally had enough of Sheila's whining and told her to climb up on the roof and fix the antenna instead of sitting on her fanny, expecting someone else to do it for her.

Now Lula is beside herself because she feels responsible for the accident."

A sliver of apprehension shot through Amanda's mind. What if . . . what if Lula, in a fit of temper, had been the one who gave her trouble-making granddaughter a shove before tramping off to tend errands? What if Lula had purposely called Amanda to establish an alibi? And what if Lula had purposely left the rake in the garden to throw Amanda off track?

Surely not, Amanda told herself. Although Lula strongly disapproved of Sheila's indolence and her wild ways, she would never bump off her own granddaughter . . . would she?

Amanda grimly reminded herself that domestic quarrels had led to many an unfortunate crime. Anything was possible.

When Thorn brushed past to climb onto the tractor, Amanda grabbed his arm to detain him. "About tonight . . ."

Nick glanced down at her. "Are we off or on again?" he asked her.

His voice hit a husky pitch that vibrated across Amanda's nerve endings. She couldn't stay mad at Tom Selleck's clone— minus the mustache. Even if Thorn did occasionally annoy her to the extreme, she was crazy about the man. With their hectic work schedules there was little time for privacy. Furthermore, she knew Thorn had been doing double duty lately, trying to catch up on his extra work, because he was farming twice as much ground. Amanda would simply go about her investigation and let Thorn do his own thing.

"We're on, Thorn," she announced.

Amanda was rewarded with a quick but passionate kiss that indicated Thorn's motor had begun to idle faster than his tractor.

"See you at supper, Hazard," he growled seductively.

When the tractor lurched off, Amanda stared after it. She was going to stop being so hard on Thorn, she promised herself. He was up to his neck in work during his vacation from police duty. She would simply carry on in the name of truth, justice, and the American way.

It was her third case, after all. She could handle it by herself, she thought confidently as she headed toward her car. All she had to do was dig up background information at Last Chance Cafe and Velma's Beauty Boutique and dream up excuses to question her suspects. When all the groundwork had been laid, she would call in Thorn and present him with the undeniable facts.

Amanda showered, changed, and scheduled her appointment with Velma. She was on her way out the front door to spend the evening with Thorn when the phone rang.

"Hazard's house."

"Hazard, stay put. Lock all your doors and

windows and don't open up under any circumstances."

Amanda frowned at Thorn's authoritative
voice. "What's the problem?"

"Deputy Sykes called on the CB to report that
a convict escaped from the federal reformatory
early this afternoon. No one knew he was missing until an hour ago."

Another suspect to add to the list? Amanda
mused. She hadn't thought to ask if anything
was missing from the MacAdo house. Yikes! The
fugitive could have gotten away with murder
and no one except Amanda was any the wiser.

"The inmate climbed out through the heat
and air conditioning ducts," Nick reported hurriedly. "He stole some clothes and hot-wired a
pickup. A highway patrolman tried to pull him
over for speeding, but the felon tore off on a
high-speed chase on country roads. The fugitive
finally ditched the truck and took off on foot,
headed in your direction. He stole a rifle from
Clive Barnstall's farm this afternoon, too."

Amanda gulped. Clive's farm was near the
MacAdo residence. The convict could have been
lurking around the area while she was delivering
her canned beans and peaches to Lula!

"Don't even think about going outside to feed
the animals tonight," Nick ordered. "I want you
in one piece, not a hostage with holes blown in
your gorgeous hide. The man might turn desperate while he's being hunted."

Sometimes Amanda loved it when Thorn got all forceful and possessive. "Bless you, Thorn."

"We'll start surveillance around your farm-house as soon as I can get the helicopters and black-and-whites over there."

The line went dead and Amanda glanced apprehensively toward the window. It was almost dark and there were dozens of places for a jail-bird to nest. Thus far, she hadn't heard the pigs squealing or chickens clucking. Pete, the three-legged dog she had inherited from Elmer Jolly, was sprawled on the front porch taking a snooze. Surely her critters would have alerted her if someone was skulking outside . . .

Just then, Pete let out a bark to raise the dead and scare the pants off the living. Amanda shot off to lock the doors and windows. So much for subtly grilling Thorn for information on the murder case. The fugitive could be looming outside her house, armed with Clive's rifle, ready to murder *her.* Could the same fugitive have been the man who sent Sheila toppling off her ladder to ensure her silence before he made off with ready cash?

In a matter of minutes, the sounds of sirens blared in the descending darkness. Bright beams of light swished across the lawn, illuminating the tin barn and hog shed. Headlights gleamed as the brigade of patrol cars zoomed up and down the country roads. Heavily armed policemen poured out of a van to search the wooded creek west of the house.

My goodness, the county law officials had arrived in full force! It didn't take a genius to realize this fugitive was not only armed, but potentially dangerous. Who the hell was he? A mass murderer on the loose? Thorn hadn't bothered to say. Probably to prevent scaring her to death— if the vicious serial killer didn't get her first.

Amanda tensed when she saw Thorn's squad car skid around the corner of the driveway. Armed to the teeth, spotlighted by two copters hovering overhead, Nick stalked toward the barn to investigate.

A tingle of pride rippled through Amanda while she watched Thorn check every shed and outbuilding on the premises. He was all business, risking his life to protect her from the rough, violent elements of society. She had never considered herself the overly romantic and sentimental type, but seeing her hero prowling around in the dark softened her feminist veneer. It had been a long time since a man had tried to protect her from anything.

Maybe it was high time Amanda introduced Thorn to Mother. If he was bold enough to take on an escaped con, he could surely handle Mother. She was tough, but she wasn't *this* dangerous.

While copters loomed overhead, their blades swishing like gigantic scissors, Amanda aimed herself toward the kitchen. Thorn would probably work up a voracious appetite, what with all this physical exertion to protect her from harm.

Amanda plucked up two cans of tuna from her alphabetically arranged cabinets and started to work. When Thorn came inside, she would have a hot meal awaiting him . . .

The kitchen door rattled abruptly and Amanda dived to the floor, her chin scraping the aged linoleum. Her heart nearly beat her ribs to splinters before she recognized Thorn's brawny silhouette through the glass.

"Open up, Hazard, It's only me."

Amanda pulled herself together and scraped herself off the floor. When she opened the door, Thorn swooped down to give her a huge kiss.

"You okay?"

"I am now," she said breathlessly.

"I'm on my way to check the chicken house and pigpen—"

Amanda flung her arms around his neck and proceeded to squeeze the stuffing out of him. Pressing ever closer, she planted her lips on his and sucked the breath clean out of him.

"What was that for?" he asked when she allowed him to come up for air.

"Every time I see you in action it impresses the hell out of me, Thorn."

He waggled his dark brows and stepped back. "Hold that stimulating thought for the next few hours and I'll see if I have enough energy left to impress you in more intimate ways."

Then his rakish grin faded and he became serious. "Keep the door locked for everybody except me, Hazard. If the fugitive manages to overtake one of the patrolmen and swipes his uniform, I don't want him bluffing his way in here to get his hands on you."

"Got it, Thorn. Don't mess with any man except you."

He smiled at the double meaning and at the fact that Hazard had finally accepted their relationship for the good thing it was. "I'm going to run the infrared heat detector down the creek and culverts. If nothing turns up in the next hour, this place will be declared safe. I, of course, will be spending the night here to ensure your continued safety. Any complaints about the arrangement, Hazard?"

Amanda smiled wryly. "No complaints, Thorn. But I would like to know if you always keep potential hostage victims in your protective custody."

Nick grabbed the doorknob to let himself out. "Nope, only sexy blond bombshell accountants. Lock the door behind me."

When Thorn marched off, Amanda whizzed into the living room. She intended to keep her mind off the possible dangers outside by thumbing through the phone book to attach numbers and addresses to the names she had heard over the CB.

Beginning tomorrow, she was going to invent ways to subtly interrogate those who might have had reason to dispose of Sheila MacAdo. She also made a mental note to have Thaddeus Thatcher mount new tires on her Toyota . . .

When a shadow flitted past the window causing Pete to bark, Amanda grabbed the pewter bookend off the table—just in case. While she waited for the search patrol to comb the area, she alphabetically stacked her magazines. She was not nervous. She did not become nervous. She was only killing time—or so she told herself.

Exactly one hour and fourteen minutes later, Thorn hammered on the front door. Amanda, still holding the bookend, invited him inside.

"We found evidence that the fugitive has been here," he told her as he propped his rifle beside the door. "The heat sensor indicated the escaped con bedded down with your chickens for a time. The sheriff's department is shifting the area of surveillance northwest."

"But you're here for the duration of the night?"

Nick nodded his raven head. "Yes, although I agreed to assist in the search at first light."

"I'll warm up dinner for us. We're having tuna on a shingle."

When Hazard whizzed by toward the kitchen, Nick detoured her toward the hall. Discarding his weapons along the way to the bedroom, he growled, "I'm not *that* kind of hungry, Hazard."

Amanda looked up into those dark, bedroom eyes and lost track of time and place. "Neither am I, Thorn." She unbuttoned his shirt to relieve him of the pistol and holster that was strapped around his broad shoulders. "Neither am I . . ."

"I'm not completely disarmed—yet," he murmured as he scooped Hazard off the floor and headed down the hall.

"I'll get to that shortly," she said with a wicked giggle.

"*Shortly,* Hazard? I think I'm insulted— " When her hand drifted down his muscled torso, his breath hitched.

"If I've hurt your feelings, I'll kiss them and make them better . . ."

Hazard, Nick reminded himself with a husky groan, could be unbelievably suspicious and cynical at times. This, however, was definitely not one of those times. She was all woman.

Although it had not been a good day, it was definitely turning out to be one hell of a good night, Nick thought . . . just before Hazard made him forget everything he ever knew.

Four

Thaddeus Thatcher swiped his hand through his mop of silvery hair and then resettled his cap on his head. "Told you so, li'l girl."

Amanda swallowed a scowl as she unfolded herself from her compact car. The fifty-year-old service station owner had been calling her "li'l girl" since the first day she pulled into his station to fill her gas tank. The smug expression plastered on Thaddeus's weathered face didn't improve Amanda's disposition. Nor was she pleased that she couldn't even have a blowout on a country road without the news reaching town before she did. But that was small-town America for you.

Thaddeus gave the spare tire on her Toyota a kick with the toe of his Red Wing boot. "I knew you were flirting with trouble yesterday. Bubba told me he picked you up after you blew your bald tire."

Before Thaddeus launched into one of his long-winded spiels on the statistics concerning motorists who suffered blowouts, Amanda gestured toward the tire rack beside the open garage door. "Are those my replacements?"

"Yep, but I had a couple of emergency jobs come up this morning. You'll have to leave your car here. We should be able to get to your car by late this afternoon. Bubba can run you home."

"Yo, Bubba!" Thaddeus trumpeted.

Bubba Hix lumbered through the garage door, wiping his greasy hands on a greasy rag. "Yeah, boss?"

"Will you give this li'l girl a lift home for me? I've got to get started on Deputy Sykes's squad car. He nearly blew his engine during the fugitive search last night."

"Have you heard any reports on the escaped inmate this morning?" Amanda questioned interestedly.

"Only that the jailbird is still on the loose," Thaddeus replied as he hiked up his drooping breeches. "There's so many wooded creeks around Vamoose that the guy could be hiding anywhere. You be careful now, li'l girl," he insisted in a fatherly tone. "I've heard the cops found evidence that the escaped con was at your place for a while last night. You never know if he might double back once your farm is declared safe."

That was not a comforting thought.

When Bubba wheeled Thaddeus's truck—laden with worn out tires— up beside her, Amanda climbed into the cab.

"You must have had one whale of a day,"

Bubba commented as he surged off. "First a blowout and then a search of your property." He glanced sideways at Amanda. "And I heard you were the one who found Sheila, too."

"Where did you hear that?" Amanda wanted to know.

"From Miz MacAdo. Me an' Sis went down to pay our respects last night. She's our closest neighbor, you know. Officer Thorn told Lula that you were the one who happened on Sheila."

Amanda rolled down the window when the fumes radiating off Bubba got to be too much for her. "How is Miz MacAdo holding up?"

"As good as can be expected, I reckon. She was in a dither when we were there. Couldn't seem to sit still. She was packing Sheila's clothes to take to the Salvation Army— organizing them by seasons, too."

Amanda nodded musingly. Here was another example of Lula's meticulous organizational habits— ones that reinforced Amanda's belief that the misplaced garden rake was a clue Thorn refused to acknowledge.

"I expect the traffic on our country road will decrease considerably now that. . . . Well, you know."

Amanda had heard the farmers in the area say something to that effect over the CB. "Needed a traffic cop out there, did you?"

Bubba nodded his oily, brown head. "Sheila was a real looker. There were always cars and trucks pulling up to the MacAdo place. Sis can see that house from the kitchen window of our trailer while she's washing dishes."

Amanda made a mental note to pay Sis a call after lunch. Sis might be able to shed some light on possible suspects.

Bubba swerved into the driveway and waited for Amanda to climb out of the truck. "Now you be careful around here, 'Manda. You heard what Thaddeus said about that fugitive circling back."

Amanda strode toward her old jalopy truck. Thorn had driven off at first light, promising to leave updated reports about the continuing search on the answering machine.

Revving the engine, Amanda wheeled her old model pickup toward town. Although she had stacks of paperwork awaiting her at the office, she was driven to pursue the niggling feeling that Sheila wasn't the victim of an accident.

Over and over again, Amanda replayed the events leading up to the discovery of Sheila's body sprawled in the melon patch. Something else had been out of place— besides the rake— at the scene, Amanda prompted herself. There was something she had overlooked that kept tapping at her brain.

She sighed heavily as she pulled into her office driveway. She would take Lula's tax forms home with her to study that evening. Maybe the financial statements would provide a clue. Follow the money, Amanda told herself. That's what Magnum P.I. usually did. Lula's painstaking tax records might pave a path for Amanda to follow.

After a quick stop at her office, Amanda detoured to Last Chance Cafe for a cup of coffee. The restaurant would undoubtedly be abuzz with discussion about Sheila's deadly mishap.

Sure enough, conversations were whipping around the booths and tables like the four winds. The place was teeming with excitement. Talk of Sheila's fatal fall warred with conversations about the escaped convict.

Amanda parked herself at a table in the center of the cafe to eavesdrop on all conversations. She inwardly flinched when Jenny Long sauntered toward her to take her order. Although Thorn had assured Amanda that he had no romantic interest in his ex-girlfriend, the bosomy brunette continued to hold a grudge against Amanda. The thought reminded Amanda of Sheila's ex-husbands.

Jenny gave Amanda the cold shoulder treatment every chance she got. Amanda wondered what treatment Sheila's ex-husbands had given *her*. A forceful shove off the ladder perhaps?

"The usual, I suppose," Jenny mumbled as she struck one of her Cleopatra poses for the benefit of the male patrons.

Amanda nodded her blond head. "Coffee with cream and sugar, please."

Without another word Jenny sashayed off, her jean-clad hips gliding like a porch swing. In less than a minute Jenny was back with a cup of coffee that had been so heavily doctored with sugar that Amanda inwardly cringed at first taste. She glanced over the rim of her cup to see Jenny smiling spitefully.

"Perfect," Amanda declared. "Just the way I like it."

The comment burst Jenny's bubble, and her mouth turned down at the corners. As she wheeled around to wait on another customer, Amanda remembered what Thorn had said about Sheila being a couple of years behind him in school— which would have made her Jenny Long's age.

Perhaps it was time for Amanda and Jenny to bury the hatchet. Jenny might be helpful when it came to providing information about Sheila and her probable murderer.

"Do you have time to sit down a moment?" Amanda asked as amicably as she knew how.

Jenny glanced down at the empty chair as if she expected to find a scorpion planted on it.

"I have a proposition for you," Amanda announced, her brain sparking an ingenious idea. She had been considering hiring a secretary to help with her work load at the accounting office. The offer might go a long way toward resolving this awkward rivalry between Amanda and Jenny.

Jenny regarded the attractive, blond accountant warily. "What are you up to?"

Amanda gestured for Jenny to park her fanny in the chair. Reluctantly, the brunette sat down.

"I would prefer to have no hard feelings between us," Amanda insisted. "After all, we do have something in common."

"We do?"

Amanda nodded affirmatively. "We do. We both are exceptionally fond of Thorn."

"But he chose you," Jenny grumbled. "Where does that leave me?"

"It leaves you in a position to let bygones be bygones. I'm in need of a secretary at my office, someone who can take phone messages, set up appointments, and file tax forms. I was hoping you might be interested in an increase in salary and shorter working hours."

That got Jenny's attention in a hurry. "A raise?"

Amanda had her now. Money was a wonderful mediator. "I know you have a young son to raise. I could offer you better hours and no weekends."

"Hey, Jen, could we have a little more coffee over here?"

Amanda glanced over to survey the man who was sitting across the aisle in a booth with Harry Ogelbee. He lifted his empty cup and smiled pleadingly.

"In a minute, Royce. We're talking business here."

Royce? Amanda appraised the man dressed in trim-fitting blue jeans, freshly starched Western shirt and expensive lizard boots. Royce Shirley? Sheila's third husband?

"I'll take the job," Jenny decided.

Amanda smiled triumphantly as Jenny scurried off to grab the coffeepot. As she breezed by, she paused to offer Amanda another cup of coffee. "Sorry about dumping all that Nutra-Sweet in your cup. It won't happen again, boss."

"Glad to hear it." Amanda extended her hand and offered Jenny a peace-treaty smile. "Friends?"

"Friends," Jenny confirmed. "I'll give my two weeks notice today."

When Jenny strode off to fill Royce's cup, Amanda silently congratulated herself on resolving her feud with Thorn's high school sweetheart. Jenny was going to be a valuable source of information. She had grown up in Vamoose and had worked at the town's hub of gossip. Chances where that Jenny could fill in missing background information on probable suspects in this investigation.

A good detective always had her resources stacked like ducks in a row.

"Sorry to hear about your ex," Harry Ogelbee said to Royce.

Amanda pricked up her ears.

Royce Shirley eased back on the seat and took a puff of his cigarette. "Yeah. That's not the way I expected Sheila to go. Lula's out at the farm right now, beating herself up, thinking it was all her fault."

Royce gave a snort and blew a smoke ring in the air. Amanda took careful note of his brand.

"Too bad Lula isn't a lot younger. I should have married her instead. I could have saved myself considerable frustration," Royce grumbled.

"Things will go a lot easier with your divorce now." Harry bit into his chocolate donut.

Royce nodded in agreement as he took another drag on his cigarette. "It will save me considerable money, too. That b— " He glanced away. "Sheila cost me an armload the way it was."

Amanda decided to introduce herself to Husband Number Three while she had the chance. Pasting on a cordial smile, she stood up and moved over to their booth. "Amanda Hazard," she greeted, sticking out her hand.

Royce perked up immediately, Amanda was quick to note, and folded his hand around hers.

"Don't get any ideas, Royce," Harry snickered as he dug into the pocket of his OshKosh overalls to leave Jenny a quarter for a tip.

Cheapskate, Amanda thought to herself. What the hell would a quarter buy these days? One lousy piece of bubblegum, and that was about it.

When Royce glanced from Amanda to Harry, the older man frowned warningly. "She's Thorn's girlfriend. You've been spending too much time in your feed store in Pronto to know that, I guess."

Royce retracted his hand and tamped out his cigarette. "Oh." But he cast one more interested glance in Amanda's direction.

"You run a feed store?" Amanda questioned. "You're just the man I need to see. I have to restock feed supplies for my chickens and hogs. My hens aren't producing as well as I had expected. Maybe they're suffering vitamin deficiency."

"I could deliver some feed on my way home from work," Royce quickly volunteered.

"I would appreciate that." Amanda batted her long lashes. She was making progress with one of the suspects.

"Well, I better get back to the store." Royce dragged his gaze from Amanda and focused on Harry. "I'll have one of the boys deliver your cattle cubes this afternoon so you won't have to climb down from your tractor to pick them up yourself."

Harry checked his watch. "Thaddeus should have filled my fuel tank by now. I guess I don't have an excuse to sit on my duff all morning."

When the two men ambled out the door, Amanda followed after them, silently congratulating herself. Before the day was out, she would collect all sorts of useful information for this case.

Amanda stood on Miz MacAdo's front porch, waiting for the elderly widow to answer the knock. Eyes misty with tears, Lula opened the door and stepped aside. If Amanda had ever seriously given thought to adding Lula's name

68 *Connie Feddersen*

to the list of suspects, she immediately removed it. Those weren't crocodile tears spilling down wrinkled cheeks, Amanda decided. They were the real thing.

"I came by to offer my condolences, Miz MacAdo."

Lula removed her wire-rimmed glasses and blotted her puffy eyes. "I just can't believe it." She inhaled a shaky breath and motioned for Amanda to follow her into the living room. "And worst of all, my last words to Sheila were sharp and abrupt. I'll never forgive myself for ordering her to climb that ladder and fix the aerial herself."

Amanda sympathetically patted Lula's sagging shoulders. After murmuring some consoling words, Amanda glanced around the room, noting everything was in its place— as usual.

"Miz MacAdo, I was wondering if I could ask you a few questions."

Lula waved her off with her used Kleenex. "Not to worry about your entries for the fair. I already labeled and stashed them in the basement."

Amanda glanced toward the kitchen, noting the canning jars were no longer sitting on the window sill. There was only the oversized tabby cat. The nagging sensations that assailed Amanda earlier that morning flittered down her spine. But for the life of her, she couldn't decide what it was that her subconscious was suggesting she had overlooked.

"I was curious to know if you had any visitors yesterday morning before you left for town."

The question caught Lula off guard. She frowned, bemused. "Well yes, I did. Why?"

Amanda sank down in a chair— the one Sheila must have been sitting in before she nose-dived off the ladder. "I only wondered who else brought fair entries by the house before you left."

"Doralee Muchmore brought her fruits and vegetables. Emma Jane Driscoe delivered a Sunday dress to be entered in the sewing competition. And Mary Kay Rutherford brought by two girl's dresses."

"Any phone calls?"

Lula thought about it for a moment. "Someone called Sheila, but she didn't tell me who it was. She was pouting because I told her to get off her tail and check the antenna."

"Did you take your purse with you when you left the house?"

Lula blinked. "Yes, I did. What has— ?"

"What about Sheila's purse?"

"Sugar, what in tarnation is this all about?"

Amanda thought fast. "I don't know if you heard the news or not, but an escaped inmate was in the area yesterday. He stole Clive's truck and rifle. I was wondering whether you noticed any missing cash." Amanda discreetly crossed the fingers of both hands and added, "Thorn asked me to check it out for him while he's conducting the manhunt."

"You think the fugitive had something to do with Sheila's fall off the ladder?" Lula croaked. "Dear Lord!"

Before the older woman dissolved into hysterics, Amanda leaned over to pat her hand. "You know how conscientious and thorough Thorn is." *Sometimes, when he thinks a case requires a full-scale investigation.* "He just wanted me to double check." *He would strangle me if he knew I was trolling for clues on his behalf.*

Lula levered out of her chair and waddled toward Sheila's bedroom. Amanda was one step behind her.

"Oh, my goodness!" Lula crowed as she dug into the purse. "Sheila's billfold is *gone!*" Wide eyed, she wheeled on Amanda. "Do you suppose that convict startled Sheila and then stole her billfold? He could use her credit cards and I'll be stuck with the bills!"

"I strongly suggest you call in the missing cards and have payment stopped immediately," Amanda advised. "Better safe than sorry, I always say."

When Lula scuttled off to look up the phone numbers for the credit offices in her orderly files, Amanda waved good-bye and let herself out of the house. On impulse, she wandered around to the garden to survey the scene of the crime once again. The rake and ladder had been removed. A quick inspection of the shed verified the fact that the tools and equipment had been returned to their alphabetized places. She wondered if Lula had been too bereaved to realize the rake had been left in the garden. Amanda was tempted to return to the house to ask Lula about it, but decided the older woman had suffered enough distress for one day.

Amanda pivoted and then stopped short when she noticed the cigarette butt that had been mashed into the grass beside the house. She squatted down to retrieve possible evidence. Sure enough, it was the same brand as the one Royce Shirley had been smoking that morning.

A frown beetled Amanda's brows as she strode to her gas-guzzling jalopy. The clues she had unearthed didn't add up to much of anything. Sheila's missing billfold suggested the fugitive might have been on the premises and swiped some cash. The cigarette butt indicated Royce Shirley, or someone who smoked his brand of cigarettes, had indeed been here sometime recently. The mysterious phone call could have meant Sheila was expecting company.

Damn, Amanda was giving herself a queen-sized headache trying to sort through the possibilities. But from what she had gleaned, she was sure someone had been at the house before, during, and probably after Sheila's death. Ten to one, it wasn't the wasps that caused Sheila's lethal fall.

Clinging to that firm conviction, Amanda veered toward the trailer house that sat a quarter of a mile from MacAdo Farm. It was time to pay

Sis Hix a visit to determine what she might have seen while washing dishes by the kitchen window.

Five

Amanda slammed on the brakes when she saw Bubba Jr. toddling toward her old truck. The kid didn't have the sense God gave a goose! She could have flattened him.

Bubba Jr. crawled onto the running board, clamped his hands over the open window and pulled himself up the side of the truck. Amanda smiled despite herself while B.J. jabbered non-stop.

"Hop down, Bubba Jr.," Amanda insisted. "I came to talk to your mama."

Still blathering, the toddler slid back to the running board and tumbled to the ground. Then he scuttled up the uneven wooden steps to the trailer to announce their guest. Before Amanda could set one foot on a rickety step, Sis Hix was at the door, looking more rounded and bustier than usual in her close-fitting T-shirt.

"Well, hi there, 'Manda. Come on in. Bubba Jr. and I were just about to have a glass of lemonade."

Amanda forged ahead, taking careful appraisal of the trailer that Bubba and Sis Hix called home. Piles of laundry lay on the divan, waiting to be folded and put away. A threadbare carpet covered the floor. The air conditioning unit seemed to be on the blink. It was hot enough inside to melt butter. It was little wonder the Hixes smelled like a sweat factory. The temperature indoors nearly equalled the temperature outdoors.

"Sorry it's so hot in here," Sis apologized as she rearranged the tendrils of mousy brown hair that had escaped her Bad Hair Day hat. The hat, Amanda decided, was one of Sis's standard articles of clothing. For Sis, every day looked to be a bad hair day. The poor woman needed an appointment at Velma's Boutique.

When Sis strode off to retrieve the lemonade, Amanda perched on the edge of the sofa beside a stack of cloth diapers. The place was an absolute pit! Cups and glasses sat on every end table. Three pairs of grungy tennis shoes were stacked beside the small TV set. Mail-order catalogs were strewn on the floor like casualties of war.

"Bubba Jr., take 'Manda a cool glass of lemonade, will you?"

To Amanda's horror, B.J. toddled around the corner of the kitchen. His fingers were clamped over the lip of a glass and bits of dirt dribbled into the lemonade. Reluctantly, Amanda accepted the offering and forced herself to take a small sip— from the opposite side of the glass.

"I wanted to ask you a few questions," Amanda said after she wet her whistle.

Sis appeared at the kitchen door, one hand wrapped around her glass, a Twinkie in the other fist. "Sure, 'Manda." She planted herself on the far end of the divan. "What would you like to know?"

"I wondered if you noticed any vehicles pulling into the MacAdo driveway yesterday morning."

Sis twisted sideways and glanced away. Her guilty reaction indicated she was in the habit of peeping on the neighbors. Undoubtedly, the goings-on with Sheila were better than a soap opera.

"Thorn is checking out any possible leads since the fugitive from the reformatory was reported to be seen in this area."

The comment appeared to relieve Sis's feelings of guilt. She perked up immediately. "I did see some traffic buzzing around there yesterday, but Bubba picked me up to take me to the doctor during his early lunch hour. I wasn't here all morning. We were gone for almost two hours."

"Did you recognize any of the vehicles that drove by?" Amanda set her lemonade aside when Bubba Jr. invited himself onto her lap. If the kid wet on her again, so help her she was going to . . . buy him plastic pants, even if it insulted his mother!

Sis sipped her lemonade and nodded thoughtfully. "I saw Emma Jane, Mary Kay, and Doralee come and go."

"In that order?"

Sis nodded affirmatively and chased a bite of Twinkie with some lemonade.

"Any pickup trucks? The fugitive stole one from a neighboring farm."

"Yeah, a two-toned green Dodge pulled in just before we left for the doctor's office," Sis recalled. "A white Ford was there earlier. But I was changing clothes for my appointment so I can't say for sure who else came and went."

Amanda resituated the squirming toddler on her knee and glanced at Sis over B.J.'s head. "Did you recognize either truck?"

"The Ford belongs to Hugh Wilmer who rents MacAdo farm ground. I don't know about the Dodge."

Amanda did. It belonged to Royce Shirley. She had seen him drive away from Last Chance Cafe. There were now two strikes against Hubby Number Three and one against Hugh.

"What about an old model, tan Chevy?" Amanda inquired. "That's what the escaped inmate swiped from Clive's farm. He was driving it around before he took off on foot to avoid the police."

Sis shrugged her broad shoulders. "Didn't see that one, but like I said, I went to change clothes and then left for town." She took another swallow and heaved a sigh. "Sure was too bad about Sheila. Do you think she might have met up with the fugitive or something?"

Or something, Amanda silently replied. "Thorn isn't sure. He just asked me to make a routine check while he's on the manhunt."

When Sis stood up to refill her glass, the color

drained from her plump cheeks. She sat down quickly.

Amanda frowned, worried. "Are you okay?"

Sis wiped the perspiration from her upper lip and fanned herself. "I'm feeling a little dizzy. Morning sickness, I guess." She inhaled deep breaths that caused her T-shirt to strain across her ample bosom. "It doesn't help having the air conditioner on the blink. We've all been steaming like clams in here."

Amanda, despite her tough, cynical exterior, was once again reminded that, deep down inside, she was a soft touch. Her heart went out to Sis and her family. Poorly educated and poor though the Hixes were, they were friendly, kind, helpful, and hardworking. In Amanda's opinion, they deserved a break.

Setting the yammering toddler on his feet, Amanda surged toward the kitchen. "I'll get you some more lemonade. Why don't you take a cool shower after I leave."

"I would love to, but the bathroom plumbing needs repair and Bubba hasn't had the time or extra cash to unclog the shower drain and replace the faucets. We've been bathing in B.J.'s plastic pool."

After filling the glass and surveying the view from the kitchen window, Amanda returned to the living room. "I'll take B.J. with me so you can rest."

"But I couldn't— "

"I'll call Bubba at work and have him pick up B.J. when he gets off work."

"I couldn't impose— "

"And don't worry about fixing dinner, either," Amanda insisted as she scooped Bubba Jr. up in her arms. "I'll drop by Last Chance and get some burgers-to-go."

"But— "

With a wave and a smile, Amanda took off, lugging the babbling boy under one arm. When she had deposited B.J. on the seat of the truck, he reached up to adjust the rearview mirror. All Amanda could see was his dirty little bare feet staring back at her. The kid needed a good scrubbing, she decided, and a pair of plastic pants in case he sprang another leak.

"Sit down, Bubba Jr.," Amanda ordered in her most authoritative voice. "I— "

The realization that she sounded exactly like Mother hit Amanda like a 2x4 between the eyes. Heaving a sigh, she patted the toddler on the head. "Park your carcass, kiddo. You and Aunt 'Manda are headed to the Toot 'N Tell 'Em for a few supplies and an ice cream cone."

B. J.'s stubby legs shot straight out in front of him at the mention of ice cream. He dropped on his diapered bottom beside her then commenced yammering excitedly. The only words Amanda could translate were "ice cream."

Enough said.

* * *

An hour later, Amanda scooped Bubba Jr. off the seat of her jalopy and planted him on the grass. With an armload of brown paper sacks filled to capacity, she headed for her house.

A horrified squawk erupted behind Amanda. She whirled around to see Pete, the three-legged dog, helping himself to a lick of Bubba Jr.'s ice cream cone. The toddler was beside himself.

Setting the sacks on the porch, Amanda pried the cone from B.J's fist and tossed it to the dog. The toddler wailed as if he had been stabbed.

"Not to worry, kiddo. Aunt 'Manda has a sack of goodies to tide you over until supper." She thrust her hand into one of the brown bags to fish out a lollipop as big as B.J.'s fist. The toddler quieted immediately. Bribing, Amanda discovered, was a useful motivation . . .

She suddenly wondered if bribery might have had something to do with Sheila MacAdo's demise. The seductive divorcee could have been holding any number of secrets over a half dozen men's heads. Either that or the escaped inmate had bumped off the witness on the ladder before stealing her money.

Amanda wished Thorn and the sheriff's department would track that fugitive down— and quickly. She was dying to know if the jailbird was carrying a wallet and stolen credit cards.

Once inside, B.J. was content to slobber on his sucker and amuse himself with the rubber toy Amanda had purchased for him. After she had popped the sack of hamburgers and fries in the microwave oven, she ran a tub of bath water. B.J. needed a few layers of dirt scraped off of him. His mother obviously wasn't feeling up to snuff these days and hardly had the energy or stomach to double over the pool to wrestle her son.

"Yo, B.J.!" Amanda bugled from the bathroom.

The patter of little feet resounded in the hall. With sucker in hand and a layer of sticky goo surrounding his mouth, B.J. toddled through the doorway.

"Bath time," Amanda announced enthusiastically.

Bubba Jr. squealed, spun on his heels, and took off as fast as his little legs would carry him. Amanda moved quickly and snatched the kid up before he escaped to the living room. Squawking, the youngster bucked and squirmed for release, but Amanda was nothing if not determined. It was one of her redeeming virtues— at least in *her* book. Thorn did not always agree.

Bubba Jr. dropped all protests when Amanda plunked the yellow rubber duck into the water. Armed with shampoo and soap, Amanda scrubbed the toddler until he was so clean he squeaked.

My God, she thought as she towel-dried his hair, the kid had sandy blond locks. Who would have thought it?

After wrapping B.J. into a paper diaper she

picked up at the quick stop, she stuffed his feet into a pair of her socks and hoisted him onto her hip.

"Wanna help me feed the hogs and chickens?"

Bubba Jr. babbled inarticulately, and Amanda took it for a "yes."

The chickens, perched in their shoe-box nests, cackled in greeting. Bubba Jr. cackled back and leaned out to make a grab for the closest hen. Amanda stepped back before the toddler wrung the chicken's neck.

When the fowl had been fed and watered, Amanda hiked off to check on the hogs. There she was greeted by two snorts, which B.J. delightedly mimicked. Amanda stopped short when she noticed the piece of fabric that clung to the top of the wire panel surrounding the pigpen. She glanced around uneasily, recalling the warning Thorn issued before he trooped off that morning. If the escapee had doubled back, she and Bubba Jr. were in deep shit—and not just in the pigpen!

The sound of an arriving vehicle came as a great relief to Amanda. She strode toward the driveway, welcoming any visitor who might serve as reinforcement—in case the fugitive was lying in wait to abduct hostages.

When Bubba Hix emerged from his beat-up pickup, his eyes widened in surprise. "He's clean!"

Miracles did happen, thought Amanda.

Bubba trotted over to retrieve his jabbering son and gave him an affectionate hug. "I tell you true, 'Manda, kids this age don't stay clean for long. Sis think's he's part pig. We can hose B.J. down one minute and he's out rolling in the dirt the next."

Was he implying all children were doomed to being dirty, even without bad plumbing? Amanda certainly hadn't been allowed to slug through mud and play in the dirt. Mother went into hysterical hyperventilation at the very thought of soiled clothes and dirty fingernails.

Maybe that was part of Amanda's problem. She had been deprived of grime all her life. She might have turned out better if she had been permitted to muck about like Bubba Jr. It was an interesting theory. She'd have to bring up the idea with Mother when she was feeling contrary and belligerent.

"I wancha to know Sis and I really appreciate this," Bubba murmured. "She has been a little woozy lately, and Bubba Jr. is a handful. Sis is having a hard time keeping up right now."

"I was glad to help out."

"Some folks aren't," Bubba muttered. "Last week B.J. took a notion to hike down to the MacAdo farm for a visit while Sis was losing her breakfast. Hugh Wilmer came speeding down the road and didn't even bother to slow down, much less haul my kid home where he belonged. Sis had to trot after B. J., morning sickness and all."

"I take it you don't have high regards for Hugh," Amanda questioned.

"You take it right," Bubba confirmed with a disgusted snort. "He's a two-timing skirt-chaser. Even though Hugh has a wife, it didn't stop him from paying Sheila calls while Lula was away from the house."

The comment left Amanda wondering if Hugh had phoned Sheila to set up another rendezvous while Lula was out running errands. Scratch up another black mark for ole Hugh. He might have reacted violently to whatever blackmail Sheila might have dreamed up.

"And poor Alvin Priddle." Bubba shook his head in dismay and shifted his son to his other arm. "Talk about a sucker— "

Bubba Jr. lifted his lollipop to offer his father a lick. "Not that kind of sucker, Junior. You go ahead and finish it off. I'll wait for supper."

Before Bubba lost his train of thought, Amanda give him a verbal nudge. "You were saying about Alvin? Wasn't that Sheila's first husband?"

"Yep." Bubba nodded his bushy head. "He never let go, even after Sheila dumped him. The poor guy had it bad. Every time he heard Sheila was with another man he hit the bottle and then got fighting mad."

Mad enough to take his long-harbored frustration out on the lady on the ladder? It made one wonder.

"Well, I better head home to see how Sis is feeling."

"Wait!" Amanda flung up a hand to forestall him. "I picked up burgers and some paper diapers while I was in town."

"You shouldn't have done that," Bubba protested.

Amanda flashed him a dazzling smile as she strode toward the house. Using Bubba's own words, she said, "That's what neighbors are for."

After Bubba thanked Amanda a half-dozen times for her generosity, he rumbled off with the carry-out dinner, diapers, and a few toys to occupy Bubba Jr. for the evening.

Amanda ambled into the house. She had done her good deed for the day and happened onto a few interesting tidbits of information in the process. She was making progress. It seemed that any number of people might have been out to get Sheila MacAdo.

The oversexed divorcee— by Thorn's own admission— delighted in teasing and tormenting men. The more the better, or so it seemed. Sheila might have provoked her stable of studs into a crime of passion. Any one of her lovers could have given her a shove in a fit of temper.

Of course, there was still the possibility that Sheila had been the escaped inmate's victim. And as far as Amanda knew, the fugitive was still at large . . .

The thought prompted Amanda to lock the

door behind her. She had been too occupied with B.J. to check the phone messages. Punching the answering machine, Amanda impatiently waited to hear Thorn's deep baritone voice.

"Hazard? Thorn here. It's 10:00 a.m. Still no sign of the fugitive. We've found a few tracks but there's no body to go with them. The guy is as slippery as a snake shedding skin. And speaking of skin . . . mine is still tingling after last night."

Amanda stood in her living room and blushed fuchsia.

"Gotta go, Hazard. Some vacation this is turning out to be."

The machine beeped and Thorn came on the line again.

"High noon and no escaped con in sight. Evidence shows that he bedded down beside Preston Banks's granary and must have taken off through the timbers. The old rascal is putting me through the paces. Too bad I didn't get much sleep last night and expended all my energy." Thorn's voice dropped to a husky pitch. "But you won't hear me complaining about that. I'd do it all over again."

Amanda's cheeks flushed crimson again. Nobody did it better than Thorn. That was one skillful cop.

"Damn it, Hazard, don't you ever stay home?" began the next message.

Amanda knew from Thorn's tone of voice

that, as the day wore on, his patience had worn thin.

"It's 5:00. We still don't have the escape artist in custody. At this rate I'll never get the damned field work done or the cattle moved out to better pasture."

Amanda heard Thorn's weary yawn before he signed off.

Beep.

"Amanda? This is Jenny Long. I gave notice at the cafe this morning and I can start working for you on Friday, if you like. One of the high school girls already has her application in at Last Chance and is ready and willing to work. See you Friday . . . and thanks."

Beep.

"Hi, doll. I called to remind you to send Uncle Dean a birthday card. And last time you were here, I noticed the safety sticker on your Toyota is due to be updated this month—"

Amanda turned Mother off and strolled into the kitchen to heat up the high-cholesterol burger and fries she had picked up for herself. She had just washed and dried her plate and glass when she heard a vehicle pull in the driveway. Returning her dishes to the cabinet, Amanda walked out on the porch.

Another suspect had arrived, hauling feed for her critters. Amanda watched Royce Shirley slide off the seat of his two-tone green Dodge— the one Sis Hix had spotted entering and exiting the MacAdo residence the day of the presumed accident.

Amanda appraised Royce's greeting smile. It was nowhere near as stimulating as Thorn's. But then, whose was?

"I brought your stock some feed. Where would you like me to unload it?"

Ignoring the speculative glance that took in her feminine measurements in one sweep, Amanda gestured toward the barn. "West side. I'll open the door for you."

While Royce backed past the wooden corral, Amanda jogged to the barn. Royce stepped down once again, flexed his muscles, and reached for the first feed sack.

"Thorn's girlfriend, huh?" he asked, giving her the once-over— twice.

"We're an item," she replied without her previous hesitation. Amanda had decided to quit messing with the good deal she had going. She and that heartthrob cop may hit a few snags when it came to investigating a murder, but they definitely had a thing for each other that was worth cultivating. So why fight it?

"Too bad about that." Royce heaved a fifty-pound sack over one thick shoulder and swaggered into the barn.

"I was sorry to hear about your ex-wife."

Amanda watched carefully, searching for the slightest body language that might indicate Royce's hidden feelings for Sheila. His back stiffened and he broke stride.

"Yeah, too bad about that."

Amanda decided Royce wasn't very upset about Sheila's death.

Royce dumped the sack on the concrete floor, swiped his hand through his tuft of carrot-red hair, and reversed direction. His charming smile was beginning to sag noticeably on the corners of his wide mouth. Amanda propped herself against the side of the truck to scrutinize Royce while he hoisted another sack of hog feed.

"I heard you went to see Sheila the morning she died."

Bull's eye, Amanda congratulated herself. Royce stopped abruptly and spun around to face her.

His engaging smile vanished completely. The flicker in his pale blue eyes indicated hostility. "Where did you hear that?"

"Sis Hix happened to see your truck go by while she was washing dishes. And then later when I was at the MacAdo's, I noticed a cigarette butt lying in the grass beside the ladder. It was your brand."

Royce gnashed his teeth and wheeled toward the barn.

"Well?" Amanda persisted.

"Well what?"

"Did you and Sheila get into an argument about your pending divorce?" Amanda asked instead when he came back to the truck.

"We always got into arguments about our

pending divorce. So what?" Royce snapped defensively.

"So maybe you lost your temper and gave Sheila a shove to shut her up once and for all."

Amanda flinched when Royce lifted his bulky arms as if he were about to pounce. To her relief, he put a stranglehold on the chicken feed and stalked away.

"Just what the hell are you supposed to be? Vamoose's version of *Murder She Wrote*?"

"No, only a curious accountant whose favorite client's granddaughter met with disaster. My inquiring mind can't help but wonder what really happened."

"You think I finished Sheila off?" he snorted.

"A shove of the ladder would make a fascinating *coup de grace*, wouldn't it?"

"Look, lady. I didn't come out here to get the third degree about my four-timing ex—" He slammed his mouth shut and muttered to himself.

"Four?" Amanda pounced on that with both feet.

"That's a modest estimation." Royce scowled as he toted another sack to the barn. "Sheila was a spoiled, selfish, manipulative sleaze. If you ask me, she got what she deserved."

"If she was a sleaze, what does that make you? You married her, didn't you?"

Royce spun around to glower laser beams at Amanda. "It makes me one of three fools who made the same disastrous mistake," he grumbled bitterly. "Sheila was trying to clean me out and get a cut of my feed store business. And if you think my devoted wife was keeping the home fires burning when I had to make business trips and deliveries, think again, honey. The only fire she kept burning was the one in her hot pants!"

Amanda blinked when Royce's voice hit a growling pitch. He glared down at Amanda from six feet and two hundred some-odd pounds of simmering irritation. His expression indicated he still suffered volatile emotions when the subject of his ex-wife came up.

"I would have liked to strangle Sheila several times, but I didn't."

"What was Sheila doing when you went to see her?" Amanda questioned.

"She was doing what she did best," Royce mumbled as he slammed the tailgate of his pickup shut.

Amanda made note of the abrupt, forceful movement. She could envision this stocky feed salesman doing the same thing to a wooden ladder.

"And what was it Sheila did best?" she quizzed Royce.

"Sit on her butt and whine, in hopes of getting someone to do whatever she wanted done at the moment. Sheila MacAdo made a profession of manipulating men."

"She wanted you to climb up on the roof to repair the antenna?" Amanda asked.

"Of course she did."

"And what did you tell her?"

Royce displayed a grin that could more aptly be described as a baring of gritted teeth. "I told Sheila to go f— "

"I see," Amanda quickly, cutting him off. "And she said?"

Royce's suntanned face puckered as if he were sucking on a green tomato. "She said she didn't have to do it herself, because there were plenty of men around who'd gladly do it for her— and a helluva lot better than I ever did."

It sounded as though Sheila MacAdo was an expert at goading the men in her life. She may have goaded one of them once too often.

"Just to satisfy your inquiring mind," Royce added as he circled toward the cab of the truck, "Sheila wasn't on the ladder when I left."

Or so he said, Amanda mused. Only he and Sheila knew for sure. And Sheila could hardly contest his story.

"Alvin Priddle drove up while I was there. I left, just like I'm doing now."

With a roar of the engine, Royce shot off, leaving Amanda choking in dust.

That had certainly gone well, hadn't it? Amanda had scared up a few facts— or were they clever lies meant to provide an alibi? She had also irritated Royce Shirley. Although he should be used to that by now, given what he had said about his charming ex-wife. The local Jezebel had ob-

viously been into breaking hearts, and she had
gathered a few bitter enemies in the process.

The question was: Which one of them retaliated?

Six

Amanda studied the MacAdo tax forms she had retrieved from her office. Thus far, she had come across nothing irregular that she could logically link to Sheila's demise. Amanda was kicked back in her recliner, half listening to the 10:00 news. The abrupt rap at the door brought her out of her chair. Hank, the tomcat raised his broad head and winked sleepily.

"Who is it?"

"It's Thorn. Who else were you expecting at this hour of the night?"

Amanda opened the door to see Thorn's muscular body braced against the outside wall. He looked like he had been run over by a cattle herd.

"Are you all right?" she questioned in concern.

"Hell no, I'm not all right," Thorn growled as he tramped inside to collapse in the recliner Amanda had vacated. "I ran my damned legs off today— all for nothing. The fugitive is still on the loose. He could be anywhere by now."

Amanda didn't bother to ask if Thorn wanted a cup of coffee. He looked as though he could use one. Either that or a stiff drink. Too bad she didn't have any booze in the house.

In two shakes Amanda was back with a steaming cup of coffee.

"Thanks, Hazard," he murmured tiredly.

Amanda perched on the arm of his chair. "Just who is this escaped inmate you're hunting?"

Thorn took a welcome sip of coffee. Even though the beverage couldn't compete with the flavorful brew from Last Chance Cafe, Nick was thankful for the injection of caffeine. He was dog-dead exhausted. Cautiously, he glanced up into Hazard's inquisitive expression.

"The guy's name is Joe Wahkinney. That's privileged information, so don't abuse it."

Obviously the name didn't ring a bell with Hazard. That came as a tremendous relief. Nick was sure she would get hyped up if she made the connection, and he was in no mood to debate Hazard's wild conjectures concerning Sheila's death and her relationship to Joe Wahkinney.

"What was Wahkinney in for?" Amanda wanted to know.

"Armed robbery."

"Not mass murder? Considering the intensity of this manhunt I would have thought the jailbird had been convicted of quadruple homicide or something."

"When a man has been on the inside and is desperate enough to slither through a half-mile of enclosed air conditioning ducts, there's no telling what he might do next. Joe is very familiar with this part of the country and he knows how to make himself invisible if he needs to."

"He grew up around Vamoose?"

Thorn nodded his ruffled raven head. "God, I'm so damned tired I can hardly keep my chin up. But I promised to give the sheriff's department as much of my vacation time as it takes to track Joe down. I was hoping I could talk some sense into him, if we got him surrounded." Nick took another sip of coffee and shifted to a more relaxed sprawl in the chair. "I need to get the field work finished, but I want to be there when Joe is apprehended."

"I'm volunteering to drive the tractor for you."

Wide obsidian eyes that denoted Nick's Native American heritage riveted on her. "You will?"

"Sure. As Bubba Hix says: That's what neighbors are for."

Amanda had an ulterior motive in mind, but Thorn didn't need to know that. His questionable disposition would get bent completely out of shape if he knew what she planned to do.

"I recently hired a secretary to commandeer the accounting office. That'll lighten my workload considerably."

"I appreciate the help, Hazard." He managed a suggestive smile. "I'll find a way to make this up to you when I have the time and energy."

"Maybe you could take me to the Happy Homemaker Club's ice cream social this weekend."

"Is it *this* Saturday? I need to get the calves and cows relocated to the pastures."

"I'll help with that, too," Amanda generously volunteered.

Nick eyed her warily. "Why are you being so nice and agreeable these days?"

Probably because her conscience was nagging her about the little white lies that had tripped off her tongue recently. Amanda had been firing off questions in her unofficial investigation— all in Thorn's name. If he found out about it, Sheila MacAdo might not be the only fatality in Vamoose this week!

"We're an item these days," she reminded Thorn with a cheery smile. "I'm supposed to be exceptionally nice to you. Isn't that how it works?"

"Hazard . . ." There was an underlying hint of wariness in his deep voice.

Amanda playfully patted his bronzed cheek. "Relax, Thorn. I'm only returning the favor. You risked life and limb to search my property to apprehend a potentially dangerous criminal. The least I can do is help with the field work and cattle roundup. I may not be a top-notch hand, but I'm getting more countrified by the week."

Nick set his empty cup aside and let out a wary sigh. "Thanks, Hazard. Just let me rest here for a few minutes and I'll drag my butt home and get out of your hair. I have to be up at the crack of dawn again tomorrow, unless the roadblocks snare Joe first."

Amanda eased off the arm of the chair and ambled away to put the kitchen in perfect order. When she returned a few minutes later, Thorn had konked out with Hank curled up on his lap. She didn't have the heart to wake Thorn up. He could haul himself out of the chair when he woke up. If he didn't rouse, he was welcome to the recliner. In fact, it was getting to be a very comforting feeling knowing Thorn was around. Maybe . . .

"Go to bed, Hazard," she lectured herself. She would know when the time was right for further commitment. When Thorn, of his own free will, offered to let her figure his income taxes, Amanda would know she had his complete faith and devotion. Until then, things would remain as they were . . . and things were pretty damned good.

Amanda pulled her jalopy up in front of Velma's Beauty Boutique. Anticipation sizzled through her. Now she was going to get the real scoop about Sheila MacAdo. Velma Hertzog was a gum-chewing encyclopedia of knowledge— Vamoose's undisputed authority on gossip. What Velma didn't know wasn't worth knowing.

"Hi, hon," she said, snapping her gum. Velma gestured her dyed red head toward the vacant chair. "I'll have Millie combed out and sprayed in a jiffy."

Amanda parked herself in the chair while

Velma ran a wire-tooth brush through Millicent Patch's steel-wool hair.

"I guess you've heard about Sheila MacAdo." Velma sighed audibly. Her fake eyelashes fluttered against her pudgy cheeks like butterflies. "I was afraid life in the fast lane would catch up with that girl one day. What a way to go— stabbed by a picket fence."

"That girl must have been a real headache for Lula," Millicent chimed in. "Lula is so energetic and organized and Sheila was always as lazy as a slug. I know I shouldn't speak ill of the dead, but Sheila was a genuine mess. My dear Henry— God rest his saintly soul— always said Sheila's name should have been listed on her second husband's certificate as cause of death."

So that's what happened to the second husband, Amanda mused. This was very interesting news.

"Floyd Wahkinney should have known better than to marry a woman half his age. Everybody knew Sheila was only after the widower's money."

"Wahkinney?" Amanda parroted. Good grief! "Is Floyd related to Joe?"

Both women nodded confirmation.

"Joe was Floyd's son," Millie explained.

Amanda silently fumed. She had felt sorry for Thorn the previous night because he had been working so hard. And now she had discovered that sneaky rascal had withheld information from her. He had to know she would have been interested in facts that linked the Wahkinney name to Sheila.

"Floyd used to own Last Chance Cafe." Velma snapped her gum and stepped back to survey her latest creation, smoothing Millie's hair into place. "He keeled over from a heart attack six years ago. Of course, Sheila sold the place and collected the inheritance. Joe tried to sue for the property, for all the good it did him. Sheila had made double sure Floyd named her beneficiary."

"Sheila and Joe went round and round over the inheritance, too," Millie put in. "In fact, Sheila was the reason Joe got put in the slammer."

Alarm bells clamored in Amanda's head and she leaned forward, hanging on the edge of her seat.

"Joe came storming into the cafe and tried to take cash from the register, swearing he should get something from his poor ole daddy besides that run-down house just off Main Street. You know the one, Amanda. It sits behind your office."

Amanda recalled the small, wood-frame home with its boarded doors and windows. She had always wondered why the owner didn't bulldoze the place down. Now she realized that the owner had been serving time in jail.

"From what we heard, Joe got his feathers ruffled and pulled a pistol on Sheila when she smarted off about laying claim to the gold mine cafe. Joe cleaned out the cash and stalked out, bigger than Dallas and in broad daylight."

Millicent eagerly took up where Velma left off. "Sheila, spiteful little snip that she was, phoned Officer Thorn and ordered him to chase Joey down. Thorn had no choice when Sheila insisted on filing charges. Lula tried to talk her out of it to prevent ill feelings, but Sheila sent Joe to trial and had him imprisoned."

"Then Sheila had the gall to brag about it," Velma continued. "Excuse my French, ladies, but that girl was the shits."

"Of course, Sheila spent most of Floyd's money within two years. She bought herself a fancy sports car, diamond rings, and designer clothes. You name it and she had it," Millie elaborated.

"Then, wearing her halter tops and tight hot pants, Sheila went hunting for another sugar daddy to support her," Velma added. "Sheila never worked a day in her life and she kept her record clean to the very end."

"That May-December wedding between Floyd and Sheila was doomed from the start," Millie declared. "Sheila was still fooling around with her first husband partly because the poor man still carried a torch for her. Probably always will."

"Which is why Alvin Priddle heads for the honky-tonks every weekend to booze it up." Velma shook her coiffed head in dismay. "They used to call him Rag-arm Al when he was in high school. Best baseball pitcher in Vamoose County, and the entire state, until Sheila ran him through the ringer. Al could have played pro ball, but he gave it all up and hung around Vamoose, waiting for Sheila to graduate high school so he could marry her."

"He's the mechanic at Pronto's John Deere dealership, right?" Amanda queried.

A polluting fog of hairspray clouded the salon. Amanda snatched a quick breath before her lungs clogged with fumes.

"That's the one," snapped Velma. "Al is one of the few tractor mechanics who'll still make house calls— especially ones in Sheila's neck of the woods."

Millie ruefully shook her head. "That boy has been a fool for Sheila so many times it's a crying shame. He thought he could win her back after she left her third husband."

"Do you think Sheila's third husband is grief-stricken or relieved?" Amanda wheezed in question.

"Royce Shirley was as big a fool as Alvin was, even if he has been putting on that indifferent act for everybody's benefit." Velma poked her fake fingernail against a recalcitrant strand of hair that refused to stay in place and then drowned the unruly tendril with a double dose of spray. Hairspray hung in the air like sticky raindrops. "The two of them came to blows last month when they showed up on Sheila's doorstep at the same time. She, of course, was thrilled to have her ex-husbands fighting over her."

"A shameful tease, if you ask me." Millie gave a distasteful sniff as she appraised her new do in the mirror. "The way she flounced around in those short-shorts and painted-on blouses was scandalous. Half the men in the cafe went into heat when Sheila sashayed in there."

Velma and Millie weren't painting a complimentary picture of Sheila MacAdo. No one had. The divorcee used her striking looks and sex appeal to control men. No wonder Lula strongly disapproved of her granddaughter's behavior. Amanda imagined Lula and Sheila had tangled a few times on the subjects of laziness and unscrupulous behavior.

"I heard Royce Shirley held a grudge after the divorce," Amanda spoke up while she watched Millie lever her body out the chair and make her departure.

"Held a grudge!" Velma snorted. "That's putting it mildly, hon." She motioned Amanda toward the chair. "Royce runs Vamoose-Pronto Coop and travels over four counties selling feed and grain to stockmen and farmers. When he had to make an overnight trip, Sheila wasn't home twiddling her thumbs. I swear she was a regular nympho."

Amanda sank into the chair. "Just a wash and style will do," she insisted when Velma made a grab for the scissors. "I'm letting my hair grow out." The last time she came in, Velma had given her a scalping!

Velma spun the chair around, pumped it up, and tilted Amanda backward over the sink. Amanda closed her eyes when water and shampoo bubbles dribbled down her forehead. Clenching her teeth, she endured as best she could while Velma zealously massaged her scalp, pulling out a few strands of hair in the process.

"You'll like this new herbal shampoo made from tree bark and roots," Velma insisted as she rinsed, re-lathered, and scrubbed. "It gives you the tingles."

Amanda preferred the kind of tingles Thorn provided to shampoo products. If there was one thing she could say about Thorn, it was that he was very thorough in his bedside manner.

"So . . . how's Nick?" Velma asked with a twinkle in her eyes. "I'm glad you and that handsome devil finally got together. I claim responsibility for making the match, you know."

"Thorn is fine. Busy as ever with his farming, police duties, and this manhunt."

"I wonder who that fugitive is?" Velma mused aloud. "The cops are keeping it hush-hush for some reason. I couldn't even get Deputy Sykes to tell me. Usually he spills his guts with a simple nudge."

Amanda bit her tongue. Thorn had told her to keep the information confidential. Even a crowbar couldn't pry the fugitive's name loose. So her lips were sealed, but she was still peeved with Thorn for not telling her about the Wah-kinney connection with Sheila.

"I'm surprised the media hasn't gotten hold of the name by now," Velma went on. "You know how they love to screw up the police department's business by making confidential information public knowledge with a scoop for a fast-breaking story."

Amanda nodded in agreement. She had already lost respect for the media and their lack of common sense and discretion.

"Now that Thorn is renting the land you inherited from Elmer Jolly, plus his own property, I'll bet he and that tractor have become Siamese twins." Snap, crackle came the sound of Velma's gum. "It must've been hard on him to have to investigate the scene of Sheila's accident, too. As I recall, he was one of the young men Sheila set her cap for in high school. Of course, Nick spent most of his time with Jenny before he marched off to join the marines."

Amanda did not appreciate hearing Thorn's name linked to Sheila's or Jenny's, but she kept her trap shut. She had suds streaming down her cheeks and pooling at the corners of her mouth.

"So when are you and Nick going to tie the knot, hum?" Velma demanded to know. "If I were you, I wouldn't let that sexy cop run loose too long. Somebody might snatch him up. There are a lot of Sheila MacAdos in the world, you know."

Amanda blotted the soap off her lips and said, "Thorn and I are happy the way things are going. We don't want to clutter it up by rushing into anything until we know each other better."

Velma released a gusty snort. "Why heck, hon, you can get to know each other much better when you're married."

"I—" Amanda's breath was ripped from her chest when Velma stamped on the chair's lever, hurtling her forward. It was a wonder she didn't chip her teeth on the formica counter.

"Frankly, I think it's time to hear the patter of little Thorn feet in Vamoose." POW!

Amanda nearly jumped out of the chair when Velma's gum popped like a pistol. She gathered her composure, assuring herself that she was more than satisfied to hear the patter of Thorn's size ten feet when he walked out of her house that morning.

The image of Bubba Jr. sprang to mind and Amanda grimaced. She also flinched at the thought of subjecting a Thorn Jr. to Mother. No, Amanda decided, she and Thorn weren't quite ready to talk of marriage and making babies.

"What are you doing?" Amanda squeaked when the Amazon beautician loomed over her with a plastic bottle.

"I didn't think you'd mind if I tried out this new brand of hair dye on you. It's supposed to enhance blond highlights."

"I'd rather not . . ."

Amanda's voice trailed off and she shut her eyes when Velma squeezed the bottle, shooting a lavender spray on her forehead. Large, strong hands clamped around Amanda's head, working the coloring all the way to the scalp. The potent fumes, mingling with the hairspray that Amanda had previously inhaled, were suffocating her, making it impossible to register another protest.

"You're gonna love this," Velma assured her. "And so will Thorn."

After Amanda was thrust backward over the sink to be rinsed, she was jerked upright. With a hairbrush clamped in one beefy fist and a blow dryer in the other Velma set to work. Amanda decided to fire a few questions while Velma created another of her outdated hairstyles. Inhaling a purifying breath, Amanda dug for background information that would aid her investigation.

"Do you have any idea why Lula was left to raise Sheila? What happened to her parents?"

Velma gave a disdainful snort. "Have any idea? Of course I have an idea. Sheila's mama was as much the Jezebel as her daughter. Runs in the blood, you know. When Sheila's daddy caught his wife fooling around with his best friend, the spit hit the fan. Folks whispered for years that Sheila wasn't even Gordon MacAdo's kid."

"No?"

"No." Velma popped her chewing gum. "Rumor had it that Gordon's first cousin and best buddy was the daddy."

Amanda put two and two together and smiled grimly. "Muchmore?"

"Bingo." Velma blew hot air in Amanda's

face. "Doralee and Sheila could very well be half-sisters."

No wonder there had been a fierce rivalry between them, Amanda mused. The resentments could have gone deeper than jealousy over Alvin Priddle.

"Did Doralee and Sheila hear the rumors about their parentage, do you suppose?"

"Don't know how they could've missed hearing it," Velma replied as she wrapped Amanda's hair around the brush and blasted it with the blow dryer. "Everybody in town heard the scuttlebutt. After Sheila's mom ran off to California to become a star— which she never was— Gordon hightailed it to the east coast and left Sheila with Lula. Gordon was killed in a car crash shortly thereafter and nobody knows what became of Sheila's mama. Doralee's daddy occasionally used to visit Sheila when she was a kid, but he passed on before Sheila lost her second husband."

Velma whipped the chair around to face the mirror and Amanda forced herself not to scream. Her blond hair was purple! Velma had swept it up and back, keeping it in place with enough bobbie pins to set off an airport metal detector.

Amanda clamped hold of the arms of the chair when the hissing can swooped down on her. Her nostrils filled with vapors and her eyes watered as the room became enshrouded in a suffocating fog. The ozone layer, Amanda decided, had taken another direct hit. Velma was personally responsible for destroying the atmosphere.

"This new do will turn Thorn's head," Velma prophesied.

Would it ever! Thorn would be instantly suspicious when he saw the lavender beehive piled high on Amanda's head. He would know she had been digging for facts at the Beauty Boutique.

Amanda left the beauty salon and drove directly to Sis Hix's trailer house. Sis opened the door and blinked in astonishment.

" 'Manda? What the purple blazes happened to your hair?"

Amanda stepped inside at Sis's invitation. "This is one of Velma's cosmetic calamities," she reported.

Bubba Jr., just recently up from his nap, pointed a stubby finger, giggled, and chattered in his own language.

"She does *not* look like a Kewpie doll. Besides that, it isn't nice to poke fun at people. Tell 'Manda you're sorry, B.J."

The toddler mumbled two syllables and outstretched his arms, requesting that Amanda pick him up. She complied. Damn, the little rascal was getting to her.

"I was wondering where you got your Bad Hair Day hat," Amanda said as she braced Bubba Jr. against her hip. "I'll be needing one until the purple tint wears off."

"I bought it at Thatcher's Station. Thaddeus has several styles of caps back in the corner by the office where his wife keeps books. Gertrude Thatcher has one just like mine, except hers is blue. You can borrow mine if you want."

"Thanks, but no. I have a hankering for one of my own," Amanda insisted.

When Amanda tried to set Bubba Jr. on his feet, he clamped himself around her like a boa constrictor.

"Go!"

B.J.'s demand was easily translated.

"Now, son, 'Manda has important things to do."

Amanda stared into Sis's peaked face and noted the rivulets of perspiration dribbling down the sides of her face. This tin can the Hixes called home was like a sweat box.

Amanda swore she no longer recognized herself. She had lived in Vamoose too long. The atmosphere in small-town America was turning her into a tender-hearted softy.

But that was rural life for you. Everybody was more than just a neighbor. You watched out for them and they watched out for you— like family.

"Why don't you both come with me," Amanda invited. "You can drop by to see Bubba and pick up anything you need from Toot 'N Tell 'Em."

The overheated twosome could cool off in the wind that whipped through the windows of Amanda's old jalopy truck. And with any luck,

Thaddeus would have gotten her new tires mounted and balanced by now. He was already a day behind schedule.

"Well . . ." Sis glanced around the untidy house. "I should stay here and pick up a few things before Bubba gets off work."

"To hell with the housework—" Amanda glanced down at B.J. "Sorry, kiddo. Hear those naughty words but don't you dare say them until you're at least twenty-one. Otherwise your mama will feed you soap for supper." She refocused on Sis. "Grab your thongs and let's hit the road. I'll have you back in time to spiff the place up before supper."

A grateful smile passed over Sis's plain features. "You're sure you don't mind?"

Amanda assured Sis that she didn't.

"Boy, you're nothing like Sheila MacAdo," Sis mumbled as she slipped on her shoes. "Talk about a snotty snob. She wouldn't give a man so much as a pebble to suck on if he was dying of thirst. I know I shouldn't criticize the deceased, but Sheila really was the pits as far as neighbors go. When I called Lula for a recipe, Sheila hung up on me half the time. Said her granny didn't need to associate with white trash."

Amanda gnashed her teeth. As mean and nasty as Sheila was reported to be, she probably couldn't raise a crowd at her own funeral. Folks would show up out of respect and moral support for Lula— and nothing more.

"Let's grab an ice cream cone to cool us off,"

Amanda enthused. The comment had B.J. shrieking with so much excitement that he wet his diaper again. This time Amanda set him down before they both began to smell.

After a quick change into a new diaper, the threesome whizzed off.

"Sis, I was wondering if you might be interested in a part time job for the next few weeks."

Amanda couldn't believe herself. There she went again with another good deed. First she had hired Thorn's high school sweetheart to end the rivalry and grant herself time to pursue the investigation. Now she was approaching Sis with a proposition, for no other reason than to help the young, struggling family through financial difficulty. The Hixes definitely needed extra cash to repair their air conditioner and plumbing. They were too proud to accept charity, and Amanda knew no other way to help out except offering a job. Even though she now considered herself B.J.'s honorary aunt and fairy godmother, it wasn't enough.

"A part time job?" Sis perked up immediately.

"I volunteered to drive the tractor and round up cattle for Thorn since he's falling farther behind during the manhunt," Amanda explained. "I need someone to keep house for me for the next few weeks. While I'm doing a little double duty with farming and accounting, you can keep my place in order. Of course, you can bring Bubba Jr. with you. There's no need to hire a baby-sitter. It won't be anything too strenuous, you understand. A little vacuuming, dusting, and a few loads of laundry."

"I'd be delighted! We could use the extra money to fix the air conditioner and plumbing."

Amanda was hoping Sis would say that. "Then it's settled. You can borrow my old truck to drive back and forth to work. My Toyota should be road-ready by now."

"Should be," Sis confirmed. "When Bubba came home for lunch he said Thaddeus gave him the okay to mount your tires this afternoon."

Seven

Amanda received plenty of unwanted attention when they stopped by Toot 'N Tell 'Em on the edge of town. She ignored the snickers about her purple beehive hair and licked the squiggles of ice cream that dripped off her sugar cone.

While Sis and B.J. visited with Bubba at the service station, Amanda strode toward the back office to purchase a cap to cover Velma's disaster. Purple hairdos were definitely not in vogue in Vamoose. Amanda expected to be wearing a hat until the last of the discolored tint wore off.

Perching the new cap on her head, Amanda glanced around the partially opened office door to see Gertrude Thatcher, her bifocals drooping off the bridge of her nose, poring over the station's tax files.

"Amanda! Just the person I needed to consult."

Gertrude swiveled around in her creaking chair and motioned Amanda into the room. "Have you got any idea what this crazy tax regulation is supposed to mean? The Department of Motor Vehicles keeps sending me these forms to request more forms to be filed in triplicate. I've got so much red tape around here I could wallpaper my house!"

In a matter of minutes Amanda had explained the new regulations affecting fuel dealers and the tax exemptions for diesel used by farmers.

"Tell Thaddeus that hat is on the house," Gertrude insisted. "Thanks for the consultation. I'll have our files in your office the first of next week."

With a wave of farewell, Amanda trooped off to pay for her new tires.

"There you go, li'l girl. You've got traction galore now." Thaddeus handed Amanda the keys to her car. "I had Bubba change your oil and check the tension on your belts while he was at it. Your Toyota has been given a clean bill of health."

"Thaddeus, can I ask you a question?"

"Shoot, li'l girl."

"Do you know much about tractors?"

Thaddeus frowned at the inquiry. "Some, I suppose, though my expertise is with cars and trucks. Are we talking diesel engine or propane?"

"Diesel."

"I was wondering about all those wires that are visible at the front of the tractor—"

"Having trouble with an alternator, are you?" Thaddeus leaped in— mechanically speaking. "Is the gauge light flashing? Is the battery running down?"

Not yet, Amanda said to herself. But it might soon.

"Sometimes the wiring shakes loose under the hood when the farm ground is as rough as it is now. If the alternator goes on the blink you've got problems, but it's a snap to repair. You have to remove the hood cover to get to the connections, though.

"About half of all automotive problems are electrically related," Thaddeus went on to say as he hiked up his sagging breeches.

Mr. Trivia had struck again. Ten minutes later, having listened to a detailed account of the purpose of alternators, hydraulics, and generators, Amanda strode off. She knew more than she really wanted to know about the mechanical functions of vehicles. She also knew enough to lure Sheila's first husband out to the field to repair Thorn's soon-to-be inoperative tractor. It was devious. It was sneaky. But heck, amateur detectives had to devise their own tricks of the trade.

Thorn would never even have to know that his Allis-Chalmers had been purposely sabotaged and repaired—all in the name of truth and justice.

Amanda wanted to question Husband Number One, even though the information she had received about Doralee Muchmore was highly suspicious. But Amanda vowed to leave no stone unturned, no suspect overlooked. Each and every prospective perpetrator would be interrogated.

Amanda Hazard was playing on her instinctive hunches. And despite Thorn's skepticism, Amanda's perception rarely failed her. Put quite simply, she was convinced she had a bloodhound's scent for investigation and the kind of an analytical mind to solve mysteries.

After hurriedly messing up her neatly arranged house before her new maid arrived, Amanda gave house cleaning instructions to Sis Hix. Then she adjusted the yellow cap that concealed her lavender hair and drove to Vamoose. As she reached the outskirts of town she had to decrease speed and swerve to dodge some hay bales that had fallen off the semi truck ahead of her.

Smiling in wry amusement, Amanda counted the pickup trucks that outnumbered cars parked at the cafe. A typical small-town, rural community, this was a place where you didn't need to bother with a turn signal because everybody knew where you were going. The kind of place where you could dial a wrong number and spend fifteen minutes visiting with the person on the other end of the line. Ah, this was definitely Amanda's kind of place.

Refocusing her thoughts, Amanda turned to her next order of business. After grabbing a quick cup of coffee, she intended to sabotage

Thorn's Allis-Chalmers. She had already placed a call to Alvin Priddle, requesting that he examine the malfunctioning tractor. It would never do to have the mechanic show up and have nothing to repair!

For the first time in months, Jenny Long greeted Amanda with an honest-to-goodness smile when she entered the cafe.

"The usual?" Jenny questioned amicably.

"To go," Amanda requested. Her gaze swept around the crowded cafe to see an unfamiliar couple ensconced in the corner booth. "Who's that?"

Jenny glanced over her shoulder. "You mean Hugh and Roxanne Wilmer? They live in Pronto."

Bells chimed in Amanda's mind. So this hulking, muscle-bound man was Hugh Wilmer. He was rumored to have been fooling around with Sheila. He was also the one who rented Miz MacAdo's farm ground.

"Nice biceps, huh?" Jenny snickered. "I bet Hugh works out with weights."

Amanda carefully appraised the bulky blond man who wore a chambray shirt with the sleeves cut out. Hugh didn't have a farmer's tan, she noted. Amanda suspected the copper-toned Adonis was roasted the same color all over.

"Looks like Hugh Wilmer has been hanging around the tanning salon in Pronto," Amanda observed.

Jenny nodded her head in agreement. "Hugh

was a football star at Pronto High School. A real Romeo in his younger days, too."

Apparently he still was, Amanda silently amended.

"I even went out with Hugh a few times after Nicky . . ." Jenny averted her gaze and shifted awkwardly from one foot to the other. "I always seemed to pick the losers. Thorn was the only wise choice I ever made, but I let that one slip away."

"I made one lousy choice myself once," Amanda quietly confided.

Perfectly arched brows rose. "You did? What happened?"

"I married the jerk. The smartest thing I ever did was divorce him."

"The good ones are hard to find," Jenny mumbled as she pivoted around to pour Amanda a cup of coffee— doctored just the way she liked it.

Amanda sank down at the counter and discreetly surveyed Hugh Wilmer and his mousy-looking wife. The marriage looked to be based on common interest. Hugh and Roxanne both thought he was the male version of Mary Poppins— very nearly perfect in every way. Roxanne Wilmer was gazing up at her husband adoringly. It was disgusting.

"I guess you heard the gossip that Hugh was messing around with Sheila," Jenny murmured as she set the styrofoam cup on the counter.

Amanda nodded and took a cautious sip to prevent scalding her tongue.

"In my opinion," Jenny said quietly, "Sheila was lucky Hugh didn't strangle her. He was probably relieved Sheila took a bad fall. He came storming in here last week, mad as a hornet, because Sheila was planning to raise the rent when he planted this year's wheat crop."

The alarm bells went wild in Amanda's head.

"If you ask me, Hugh was trying to romance Sheila into cutting his rent instead of raising it." Jenny braced herself on the counter and leaned closer to impart more information. "And Sheila was providing fringe benefits so Hugh wouldn't complain when she hiked up the price. Miz MacAdo hadn't planned on raising the rent, but Sheila appointed herself the MacAdo financial executive, or some such nonsense."

Jenny gave a disgusted snort. "Sheila wasn't any better in mathematics in school than I was. I don't know where she got the idea she had a head for business. At least I worked as a secretary for an oil company while I was living in the city. Sheila never worked at anything except destroying marriages and seducing prospective husbands who could afford her expensive tastes."

"Do you think Sheila threatened to rent the farm out from under Hugh if he didn't cooperate?" Amanda questioned before taking another sip of her coffee.

"I don't think, I *know*," Jenny insisted. "I overheard Harry Ogelbee and Clive Barnstall bickering about it in here. It seems Sheila tried to offer the land to both of them, in case Hugh refused to pay the higher rent. They were both looking for more ground after Elmer Jolly willed his property to you and you leased it to Nicky. As usual, Sheila was stirring up trouble among men. She was always good at that."

Amanda glanced at her watch. "Gotta go, Jenny."

"I'll be at your office bright and early tomorrow. I'll bring coffeecake for us to munch on."

Amanda hurried off. She had to reach Thorn's tractor before Alvin Priddle arrived. She had tarried too long at Last Chance, nibbling on tidbits of information Jenny provided. From the sound of things, there were several folks around Vamoose who might have liked to give Sheila's ladder a shove.

Amanda plunked down on the car seat and sped off. When she spotted Deputy Sykes's patrol car beside Whatsit River Bridge she jerked her foot off the accelerator— too late. Damn, Benny Sykes had set up a speed trap and Amanda had been snared like a bounding rabbit.

The squad car flashed like Christmas lights and Amanda pulled her Toyota onto the shoulder of the road.

Deputy Benny Sykes, attired in his neatly pressed uniform and mirrored sunglasses, strolled up to her car. He tipped back his hat and braced his hands on the door. "Any particular reason for this 701?"

Amanda mustered a smile for the gung-ho officer whom Thorn still hadn't been able to train in his laid-back image. "701, Benny?"

"701," he repeated. With a flair, he removed his sunglasses. "Speeding, Amanda. I clocked you at sixty-eight in a fifty-five zone. Is there a fire somewhere around here that I don't know about?"

Benny was also unimaginative, Amanda noted. Fires weren't the only reason folks sometimes exceeded the speed limit.

"Well actually, I'm supposed to meet the tractor mechanic in a few minutes to repair Thorn's Allis."

"Thorn is having problems with the Allis?" Benny questioned.

"Yes, and I volunteered to do the field work for him while he's tied up with the manhunt." Amanda flung Benny a placating glance. "Could we discuss this 701 later? If I don't get that tractor . . . repaired, Thorn will have something else to worry about."

"He doesn't need that," Benny responded.

"No, he doesn't." Amanda shifted into drive and kept her foot on the brake. "Anything else?"

"Else? No, I guess I'll let you off the hook this time, but slow it down, Amanda. The chief doesn't take kindly to pulling you out of roadside ditches. Try to drive reasonably and prudently, under existing conditions— "

"The kind of conditions that prevail on Commissioner Brown's rough roads? Sure thing, Benny."

With a wave, Amanda accelerated. She was running short on time. She was going to have to make tracks to beat Al to the field.

The minute Amanda pulled onto the graveled road, she mashed on the brake pedal. Dirt billowed around her like a dust devil.

Luckily, Alvin hadn't arrived early. Amanda scampered across the worked ground to reach the tractor. After Thaddeus Thatcher's in-depth lecture on the electrical charging system of engines, Amanda knew how and where to tamper with the Allis. Thaddeus had explained that the voltage regulator was the brains of the system and controlled the amount of electricity produced. Of course, she wasn't planning to burn out the whole system and spend a fortune on repairs. A loose connection here and there would produce the effect she wanted.

When Amanda saw a truck speeding toward her, she reached up to jiggle the wires between the alternator and voltage regulator. She also took time to give the cable leading to the ignition switch a tug for good measure. Now all she had to do was fling a few leading questions at Alvin Priddle while he diagnosed the tractor's problems.

Amanda critically surveyed the lanky, six-foot-three-inch Rag-arm Al as he stepped down from his truck. A grimy baseball cap shaded his once-handsome face. In Amanda's estimation Alvin

Priddle had some hard miles on him, plus he looked about three-fourths hung over. Either he had been two-stepping around the honky-tonks in the city until the wee hours of the morning or he had been drinking away his grief for Sheila . . .

Or had he been drowning his guilt in beer cans?

"Amanda?" Al's hoarse voice lent evidence to a hellish hangover. "I'm Al Priddle."

Amanda watched his brown-eyed gaze rove over her cotton shirt and blue jeans. Typical male reaction to meeting a woman, Amanda reminded herself. Before her feathers got ruffled and she found herself distracted, she extended her hand in greeting.

Although Rag-arm Al was tall and lean, she could feel the strength in his grip. This was definitely no two-hundred-pound weakling. Al could have given Sheila a shove— and made it stick.

"You said you were having a problem with Thorn's Allis," Al prompted. "What seems to be the trouble?"

Amanda threw up her hands in a gesture of futility and played dumb. "Heck if I know. I can't figure out what's wrong. All I can do is drive this thing."

"What are the symptoms?"

"It just sits here and won't do a lick of work." She hoped the strategically formulated comment would remind Al of his ex-wife. Sure enough, it did.

"Reminds me of somebody I used to know," Al grunted as he strode toward the tractor.

"Oh? Who might that be?"

Hazard, you devil you, the poor guy doesn't even know he's been had.

"My ex-wife." Al clamped his long fingers around the door latch and hauled himself into the tractor cab.

"You must mean Sheila. I was sorry to hear about her death."

Al gave a grunt that could have meant everything— or nothing.

So far no good, Amanda thought. She was going to have to nudge Al again in hopes he would discuss his relationship with Sheila.

"I'm sure Miz MacAdo is lost without her granddaughter around," she baited.

"Doubt it." Al cranked the engine and received nothing for his efforts but a whining clank. "Electrical problems, I'd guess. When was the last time you checked the battery?"

"I never check the battery. I wouldn't have a clue what to check it *for.*"

Al fiddled with the knobs while Amanda drummed her fingers on the hood. So much for being subtle, she thought. She was going to have to rely upon being direct— and probably offensive. But then, she could be offensive when she felt like it.

"I heard you went by to see Sheila the morning of her fatal fall."

"Yep." Al stepped down from the Allis. "So what?"

The man was abrupt and noncommunicative. Too much booze, Amanda diagnosed.

"So . . . some folks are wondering if Sheila might not have had a little help falling on her face."

That got Rag-arm Al's attention. He spun around to glower at Amanda through bloodshot eyes. Yep, ole Al appeared to be exceptionally sensitive about the subject of Sheila.

"And they think I knocked her down? Well, I'm not surprised," he muttered. "Everybody around Vamoose and Pronto thinks I'm carrying a torch for that woman, even after all these years. I've been ribbed about it until I've grown calluses."

Not very thick calluses, Amanda noticed. The man was all bluff. When Alvin wheeled toward his truck to retrieve his tool box, Amanda was on his heels, relentless as a pit bull. "But you never really got over Sheila, did you? You kept coming back, trying to convince her to begin again— "

Amanda retreated a step when Alvin rounded on her, his waxen face puckered in a scowl. "What's with you, lady? I came out here to fix this damned tractor for Officer Thorn and all you can talk about is Sheila. Was she a friend of yours or something?"

"Her grandmother is one of my favorite clients. There is reason to suspect Sheila was the victim of more than just an accident, given the flurry of turmoil surrounding her."

"Why? Because of all the men, you mean?" Al swore under his breath as he jerked the tool box off the truck bed. "I suppose you and some of the gossiping ole biddies around here have decided one of us did her in. Well, it wasn't me!"

That's what everyone said, but Amanda refused to be deterred from her investigation. "And what was it that you argued about with Sheila that fatal morning, Alvin?"

Alvin stalked back to the tractor. "Mind your own damned business."

"Was it the fact that Sheila had been seeing someone else and you resented it?"

After momentarily breaking stride, Alvin kept right on walking. Amanda was fairly certain her shot in the dark had struck its target.

"Did you demand that Sheila stop seeing Hugh Wilmer? Or was it somebody else? Did she refuse? You know she had her own particular use for Hugh. They did business together, among other things."

Alvin dropped the tool box and spun around. He growled several oaths that would have offended Mother's priggish ears. "All right, Miss Busybody. You want facts? Then I'll give you some. Yes, I went to see Sheila. And there she was prancing around in front of Royce Shirley. It made my blood boil to see them together after she just got through telling me—the night before—that she had never loved him the way she loved me, that he had been as big a mistake as marrying Floyd Wahkinney. She always claimed Floyd was like the father she never had, or some such crap. Royce, supposedly was more financially stable than I was at the time, or she would have come back to me."

Talk about keeping a man on a string! Geez, Sheila was a master of the tactic. And poor ole Al had been so love-sick that he swallowed that nonsense—hook, line and sinker.

"She used you, Alvin," Amanda said quietly. "From the sound of things, she always did. She let you think you had a chance of winning her back."

He flung himself around to unhook the hood cover. His taut shoulders drooped. Al heaved an enormous sigh and stared at the engine without seeing anything.

"I figured that out for myself that day," he muttered, dejected. "For twelve lousy years I kept swallowing all her excuses, feeding on the scraps of her affection. But I asked her to marry me again that day."

Amanda watched Alvin check the cables and wiring with angry jerks and tugs. "And what did Sheila say?"

He tensed up as if an electrical current were sizzling through him. "She said she had considered it, but she just couldn't tolerate my drinking. Hell, she was the reason I drank! Then she told me she had too many arrangements to make to even consider marriage at the moment. She said if I cleaned up my act we would discuss marriage later."

Another stall, Amanda deduced. Sheila was a vamp and Alvin had been so crazy in love that he couldn't walk away without looking back. It was like being electrocuted and not being able to let go of a live wire.

"And then you quarreled with her," Amanda speculated. "Pleaded, too, I suppose."

Alvin unhooked all the cables from the alternator and voltage regulator and began refastening each one with swift, practiced efficiency. "I told Sheila I was never coming back and she could find herself another huckleberry. I wasn't going to be around when she had a free night and didn't know what to do for entertainment. She gave me that cocky smile of hers and told me she wouldn't have trouble replacing me. She also laughed and said I should look up her cousin Doralee, because she had been pining away for me all these years, the same way I'd pined for Sheila. She claimed two losers like Doralee and I deserved each other. And then I . . ."

Alvin bent his head over the engine and worked industriously.

"And then?" Amanda prompted him.

Alvin threw her a sideways glower and stamped toward the tractor cab. With a jerk on the fuel injection knob and a twist of the key, the Allis growled to life. After checking all the gauges, Alvin gave the Allis a clean bill of health.

"Charged and ready," he declared, stepping down.

"Thank you. Thorn will be relieved."

Alvin heaved the tool box off the ground and stared long and hard at Amanda. "Tell me something, will you?"

Rats, Amanda said to herself. She had wanted it to be the other way around. "What do you want to know, Alvin?"

"Are you as much of a pain in the ass when Thorn is around?"

Amanda tried to look properly offended. "I like to think not!"

Alvin pulled his cap down so low that his ears stuck out. "I hope not. If you are, I don't know why Thorn would bother with you. You may be a knockout in blue jeans, but you can be a little hard to take on a churning stomach, what with all your prodding questions."

As Alvin stalked toward his truck, Amanda called after him. "Send the repair bill to me, not to Thorn."

Slowly, he turned to face her, his bushy brows lifting curiously. *"You're* paying?"

"Yeah, I'm kinda funny that way. If I broke it, then I should be the one to pay for fixing it. Now, you were about to tell me what you did when Sheila cut your pride to shreds."

"I said good riddance and I left."

Well, Hazard, what did you expect to get from him? A complete confession?

"Did you see anybody else approaching MacAdo Farm when you drove off?"

Alvin gave a rude snort. "Yeah, as a matter of fact I did."

"Who?"

"Don't know." Alvin replaced his tool box and opened the door of his truck. "There was a vehicle speeding down the road from the north and another one coming from the west."

"Cars or pickups?"

"Can't say. All I could see was a cloud of dust as I drove east. Besides that, the bar ditches are so full of weeds they blocked my view."

Thank you, Commissioner Brown, you lazy old goat. Send out the mowing crew once in a while, why don't you!

"Did the vehicles pull in the MacAdo driveway?" Amanda asked.

"Don't know that either. I didn't bother looking back."

Of course not, criminals are notorious for making fast getaways.

When Rag-arm Al drove off, spitting gravel and throwing dust, Amanda's shoulders slumped. Thus far, all she had accomplished was convincing herself that every possible suspect had equal opportunity and motive to do Sheila bodily harm.

Royce Shirley was battling to keep his bank accounts and property after his divorce. Alvin Priddle was still chasing after a woman he had never completely gotten over, a woman who had led him on and then trampled on his ego. And Joe Wahkinney had a criminal record because of his conflict with his young stepmother.

Amanda had yet to make contact with Doralee Muchmore, but the woman had even more motive. Sheila had stolen Doralee's one and only love and ruined him for life. The two women had been rivals since their teenage years and perhaps they were even fathered by the same man! Furthermore Doralee would now inherit all Miz MacAdo's property when she was called to the pearly gates.

And then there was Hugh Wilmer, who'd had an affair with Sheila— an affair he obviously preferred to keep quiet, though it had become common knowledge. The only ones Hugh seemed to have fooled were himself and his moonstruck wife.

There was no telling what Sheila might have said to anger Hugh when he showed up that morning. Amanda frowned pensively as she walked toward the tractor. She was still mulling over the sequence of events leading up to Sheila's death. MacAdo Farm must have been busier than Grand Central Station that morning. Vehicles had been seen approaching from all directions.

If Sheila was alive when Alvin arrived and Royce departed, who was to say Royce hadn't doubled back later? Or maybe Alvin had considered the same tactic when the coast was clear. And who, Amanda wondered, arrived at the farm while Sis Hix was away from the kitchen window? Who arrived after Alvin made his departure? Was it Hugh? Or Doralee, maybe? Could they have found Sheila dead and kept quiet for fear of becoming a suspect? Damn it, who sent Sheila sprawling in the melon patch?

Amanda threw up her hands in exasperation and cranked the tractor. For the next several hours she went around in circles, doing the field work and struggling to put the facts and speculations in logical and chronological order.

By the time the sun sank behind the horizon, Amanda was sporting a throbbing headache. She was no closer to solving the crime Thorn had dismissed as an accident than she was when she opened her private investigation. And worse, she kept wondering if sleazy Sheila even deserved to have the truth discovered.

Truth was always the best, Amanda nobly reminded herself as she rubbed her numb fanny and wobbled toward her car. It was the American way— or at least it was supposed to be.

Amanda grimaced at the thought of the fibs she had told in her attempt to investigate. She wondered what price she would have to pay for voicing those white lies. God might be compassionate enough to overlook her methods of interrogation.

Amanda wasn't too sure about Thorn, though.

Eight

The loud thump on the front door of Amanda's recently cleaned house— thanks to Sis Hix— sent Amanda scrambling to grab a towel to cover herself. She had just stepped out of the shower.

Armed with the bathroom plunger— just in case Joe Wahkinney had doubled back— Amanda cautiously approached the door. "Who's there?"

"Who the hell do you think it is at this time of the night? Damn it, Hazard, open the damned door before I break the damned thing down!"

Wow, thought Amanda, four curse words in one breath. Thorn obviously wasn't in the best of moods. Even Hank the tomcat ran for cover at the sound of Thorn's booming voice.

Amanda unlocked the dead bolt and stepped back to admit the surly country cop who looked as if he hadn't bathed, shaved, or slept for two days. Midnight black eyes drilled into her like riveting bullets from the Beretta 96F that hung in the holster on Thorn's lean hips.

When Thorn noticed the lavender tint to Amanda's hair, a scowl twisted his lips. She mustered her brightest smile to deflect his stormy glare.

"Bad day, Thorn?"

"You did it, didn't you?"

Amanda tried to look properly affronted. "Without *you*, Thorn? Of course not. We're an item now, remember?"

"Cut the crap, Hazard," he snapped irritably. "You know exactly what the hell I'm talking about. You went right ahead and opened an unofficial investigation after Sheila's death, knowing damned well I turned in my report and closed the case."

Thorn stalked closer, his hot breath rushing over Amanda like a blasting blow dryer. "Imagine my surprise when Royce Shirley hit me up at Last Chance Cafe about sending *you* to interrogate him."

Amanda muttered under her breath. That big tattletale. Who would have thought Royce would have blabbed to Thorn.

"And imagine my further surprise when Alvin Priddle left a message on my answering machine declaring that he wasn't going to repair my Allis ever again if he was going to be given the third degree by my nosy girlfriend. Hell! I didn't even know the Allis broke down!"

An aggravated frown puckered Nick's handsome features and his dark brows formed a single line above his glittering eyes. "The Allis wasn't on the blink at all, was she? You tampered with her on purpose, didn't you, Hazard?"

"Well, I—"

"And you've been to Velma's Beauty Boutique gathering gossip and hearsay to support your suspicious theories. Hence the purple hair."

"I needed—"

"When I stopped by Thatcher's Oil and Gas, Bubba told me you'd been out to visit Sis and had hired her as your housekeeper. According to Bubba and Sis, you're questioning the fact that Sheila's death was the simple accident everybody thought it was."

"Thorn stop interrupting me and let me speak—"

"Why? From the sound of things, you've been speaking for *both* of us!"

His voice hit an angry pitch that reminded Amanda of a sonic boom.

Nick stamped a step closer, shoving Amanda's bathroom plunger aside to wag a lean finger in her face. "Now you listen to me, Hazard. I've got enough trouble trying to track down Joe Wahkinney and reason with him before some of those trigger-happy rookies from the sheriff's department drop him in his tracks. Joe never got a break in his whole damned life. I intend to be on hand to ensure he lives long enough to get one this time. I do not need you stirring up gossip, igniting tempers, and getting Vamoosians all riled up for nothing!"

"Thorn, lower your voice before you crack my good crystal."

"Damn it, Hazard!"

The tomcat yowled in the hall and Amanda rolled her eyes. "Well, there goes Hank's sensitive feline eardrums."

"To hell with Hank! I want this stopped," he blared at close range.

"Thorn, you really should calm down," Amanda insisted, adjusting her droopy towel. "Your blood pressure will soon be shooting through the roof. And furthermore, my investigation has turned up some interesting facts."

"Juicy gossip is more like it," Nick grumbled in correction.

"Let me fix you a cup of coffee and we'll discuss the investigation."

"There is no investigation and your coffee tastes like tar. And don't offer me any pacifying snacks, either, because I'm perfectly content chewing on you."

Three months ago Amanda would have lashed back at Thorn in retaliation. After firing insults at twenty paces they would both have stormed off, refusing to speak to one another for several days. But now that they had a relationship going, Amanda had made a pact with herself to resolve problems rather than letting them fester. Besides that, she was crazy about this sexy country cop, even though he was presently suffering from a surly disposition.

"I have discovered that several people around

Vamoose and Pronto had plenty of motive and ample opportunity to do Sheila MacAdo in," she said with firm conviction.

Nick plopped onto the sofa. "Get me some aspirin, Hazard," he demanded with a tired sigh. "If I have to hear this, and it appears that I do, I need something to soothe this splitting headache."

"You know I don't keep aspirin around the house, Thorn. It upsets my stomach."

"Then find something equally potent. I'm saying yes to drugs tonight," Thorn mumbled, massaging his throbbing temples.

Amanda gave him a consoling pat on one muscled shoulder and pivoted toward the kitchen. "Yes, dear. I'll see what I can find to relieve your headache."

"Hazard?"

"Yes, Thorn?"

"I forgot to tell you that you look especially tempting in that towel."

Amanda smiled to herself and mimicked Jenny Long's drumroll walk. Thorn whistled wolfishly.

"Forget the drugs," he growled as he snaked out his hand to tow her back to him. "I have a better remedy for this skull-jarring headache—"

The phone shrilled and Nick groaned. Reluctantly, he released his grip on the towel and reached for the telephone. "Hazard's house."

"Thorn? Is that you, or has Amanda found

another boyfriend who has the courage to come and meet the family?"

"Hello, Mother. You seem to be as charming and tactful as ever." While Thorn and Mother exchanged civilized insults, Amanda scurried into the kitchen to retrieve some medication for Nick. She yelped in dismay when she opened the cabinet door, finding her alphabetically arranged supplies in total disarray.

Bubba Jr.'s handiwork, no doubt. That wild little rug rat made messes faster than Sis Hix could clean them up. No wonder their trailer house was such a pit. The kid was worse than an Oklahoma tornado.

"Hold on, Mother." Nick dropped the phone and dashed into the kitchen when he heard Hazard scream. He expected to find her being held hostage in her skimpy towel by the desperate Joe Wahkinney. Instead, he found Hazard staring at the contents of her cabinets.

"What the hell's wrong?"

"Look at this kitchen!" Amanda gestured toward the shelves and then clutched at the towel that slid to her waist.

A devilish grin kicked up at the corners of Nick's mouth. "I'm looking. You've got great appliances, Hazard."

Mother could be heard squawking on the phone. She still hadn't shut up. In resignation, Nick wheeled around and walked back to the living room.

"A problem?" he repeated when Mother yammered in his ear. "Not exactly. Hazard's house-keeper has a young son who de-alphabetized the kitchen cabinets. It took your daughter by surprise, is all. Her scream is nothing for you to be alarmed about."

"House cleaner?" Mother snorted. "Since when did Amanda hire a maid? She never said anything about it to me."

"I wasn't aware she had to clear it with you first. Obviously she wasn't either."

"Don't get sarcastic with me, Thorn. If you intend to worm your way into the Hazard family's good graces, I advise you to watch your mouth."

"Sorry, Mother, I have a horrendous headache after being on a manhunt for the past three days and most of the nights."

Wearing her towel like a grass skirt, Amanda sauntered back into the living room to offer Thorn a glass of water and Tylenol. While Mother chattered incessantly about the Labor Day picnic, demanding that Nick finally show his face, he feasted on the appetizing scenery.

"Excuse me, Mother, I hate to cut in but I have to take my medication."

"Then let me speak with Amanda," Mother demanded.

"Sorry, but she's the one administering my medication."

Mother obviously didn't like the sound of that. She was still yowling when the receiver was plunked back into place. Nick promptly switched on the answering machine.

"Let's discuss my investigation, Thorn."

Nick grabbed her free hand and tugged her down onto his lap. "The one that began with a garden rake, right?"

"That's the one," Amanda confirmed, her voice quavering from the effects of Thorn's seductive frisking.

"Okay, Hazard, you win," Nick conceded in a gravelly purr. "You can continue this unofficial investigation if it makes you happy, so long as I get to continue my investigation."

Amanda smiled when she realized Thorn was softening up in some places— and hardening in others. "Does this mean you aren't mad at me anymore?"

"Mmm, yes. I'm only mad about you now . . ."

"Thorn . . ." Amanda shifted sideways. "Your pistol is stabbing me."

A throaty masculine chuckle escaped Thorn's lips. "Not yet it isn't . . ."

Amanda's breath wobbled beneath the onslaught of tantalizing kisses and caresses that scattered her well-organized thoughts in a thousand different directions. "I was talking about your Beretta," she managed to get out— barely.

"*I* wasn't . . ."

Amanda smiled when Thorn waggled his brows and stretched out beside her on the divan. She had the feeling they weren't going to have much time to discuss the investigation or man-hunt for a good long while.

Sure enough, they didn't. But Amanda wasn't complaining. There were some things that could be put on hold— like her investigation— but this sexy cop was no longer one of them.

Amanda stopped short when she rounded the corner of her office to see Jenny Long, dressed in a conservative navy blue business suit and matching pumps, waiting beside the locked door. In stunned surprise she watched Jenny smooth the collar of her silk blouse and strike a sophisticated pose.

"I have decided to turn over a new leaf and set my expectations toward a higher class of losers," Jenny announced. "Today is going to be the first day of the rest of my life."

"You look wonderful!" Amanda complimented her new secretary.

Jenny beamed in response and ran a hand over her carefully coiffured hair. "I had Velma do my hair to give me that professional look."

"Too bad I didn't think of that," Amanda muttered.

Jenny frowned. "Come again?"

"Nothing." Amanda unlocked the office door and motioned Jenny inside. "Our first order of business is to familiarize you with my filing system."

"Everything alphabetized, from file to contents, right?" Jenny asked.

"Right," Amanda confirmed. "How'd you know that?"

"Because that's you. Organized, methodical, alphabetical. Everybody in Vamoose knows that."

Just like Lula MacAdo, Amanda thought to herself. And despite Thorn's skepticism, that out-of-place garden rake provided a vital clue. And damn it, something else had been out of place at the MacAdo Farm. Amanda wished the hell she could remember what it was. It was driving her crazy!

While Amanda thumbed through the file cabinet to retrieve the reports that needed to be typed up for Thatcher Oil and Gas, Toot 'N Tell 'Em, and Last Chance Cafe, Jenny scurried back to her car. She returned with an iced coffee cake, cups, and a coffeepot. Amanda's mouth instantly began to water at the aroma of freshly baked food. All she'd had for breakfast was Thorn— without icing. He, of course, had been scrumptious, but Amanda's stomach was growling nonetheless.

"I whipped this up this morning." Jenny set the cake and coffeemaker on the table in the corner. With the swift efficiency that would have done Betty Crocker proud, Jenny sliced the cake and set the coffeepot to perking. That done, she strode over to view the files Amanda had spread out on her neatly organized desk.

"All these financial figures have to be accurately transferred to the state and federal tax forms and then copied— in triplicate," Amanda instructed in a businesslike tone. "These figures of income and salaries are strictly confidential."

"Got it," Jenny said with a nod.

"No leaks of information to the cafe or beauty shop, no matter how much you're prodded."

"Girl Scout's honor," Jenny faithfully promised. "I won't divulge the information to a living soul."

Amanda set the notepad beside the phone. "Have the messages listed by time, client's name, and their phone number for my return calls."

"Not alphabetized?"

"No," Amanda said. "My clients should be listed in the order the calls were taken. My policy is that the early bird— not necessarily the big bird— gets the accountant."

The bell above the door tinkled and Thorn appeared. Surprise registered on his bronzed features as he appraised Hazard's new secretary and her professional wardrobe. Then shock set in. Amanda noticed Thorn's wary reaction immediately.

"I hired Jenny as my secretary," Amanda announced enthusiastically.

Silence. The only sound to be heard was the gurgle and hiss of the coffeepot.

"Will Nicky be wanting his tax files?" Jenny asked quite professionally. "I'll be glad to get them for him."

"Thorn is not on file." Amanda gave him a dirty look.

Jenny blinked her carefully made-up eyes. "Whyever not?"

"Yeah, Thorn, whyever not?" Amanda chimed in.

Nick spun on his heels, avoiding the question. "Hazard, I need to speak privately with you. Come outside for a minute, will you?"

Leaving Jenny to get situated at the computer, Amanda strode outside.

"I came by to tell you the Allis is fueled and ready. I left the diesel gas tank in the back of my old truck and parked it beside the gate so you can refuel the tractor yourself."

"I'll be in the field as soon as I get Jenny squared away," Amanda affirmed.

"What's with this secretary business, Hazard?" Thorn questioned dubiously. "I thought Jenny was suffering a severe case of female rivalry. At least she was the last time you and I dined at Last Chance Cafe together."

"Jenny and I worked all that out," Amanda said with a dismissing flick of her wrist.

Nick frowned suspiciously. "Oh?"

She hated the way he said that word. His voice carried an undertone of obtrusiveness that suggested Amanda's scheme couldn't possibly be as effective as she thought it would.

"Just leave it to me, Thorn. Jenny and I won't have any more problems. I have everything under control."

"When I leave things to you they usually get out of control— investigatively speaking." Thorn studied Hazard for a long, ponderous moment. "What role does Jenny play in whatever clever scheme you've dreamed up to track down Sheila's *supposed* murderer?"

"Informant," Amanda replied, undaunted. "She knows everybody in town, she went to school with Sheila, and she dated Alvin, Royce, and even Hugh."

"So did I, Hazard," he grumbled.

"You dated *men* in high school? Geez, Thorn, you should have said so."

"Don't be cute, Hazard— "

"Thorn, this is the sheriff's department," Nick's two-way radio blared through the open car window.

Nick strode over to answer the incoming call.

"Thorn, here. What's up?"

"The sheriff said to tell you that he has a promising lead on the fugitive," the dispatcher reported. "They have a 11-54 four miles north and six miles west of Vamoose. The fugitive was seen on foot— armed. Patrols are sealing off the area."

"I'm on my way."

Nick sank down behind the steering wheel and Amanda impulsively trotted over to give him a kiss, right smack dab on Main Street.

"Be careful, Thorn."

Nick glanced around to see Velma Hertzog strolling out of the cafe, her eagle eyes homing in on him and Hazard. The hefty beautician beamed in satisfaction and gestured two thumbs up.

"We kiss and she tells," Thorn murmured. "Can you deal with that, Hazard?"

"To hell with the gossip, Thorn. Just watch your step. You've become a habit I'd rather not see broken or shot to pieces."

"Ditto, Hazard. And don't get yourself into unnecessary trouble with this unofficial investigation, because I may not be around to protect your fabulous fanny."

When Thorn whizzed off with siren shrieking, Amanda returned to her office. To her satisfaction, she saw Jenny Long perched at the computer keyboard. Jenny may not have been rocket scientist material, but she obviously knew her way around a computer keyboard and programs. Amanda was impressed.

"I'm leaving you in charge," Amanda announced, grabbing her purse. "I'll come back from the field about noon to see how you're managing."

"I'll be here, working away." Jenny leaned over to pluck up her lunch pail. "I brought a Reuben sandwich for you, too."

Amanda walked away, smiling in satisfaction. She had lost a female rival for Thorn's affection and gained a competent secretary. Amanda was settling into Vamoose quite well. She was no longer considered an outsider, but rather one of the natives.

Now, if only she could solve this perplexing case that, as Thorn was quick to point out, over and over again, hinged on a garden rake. Amanda was going to feel like an absolute idiot if her intuition failed her. After she had solved two cleverly arranged murder cases, her reputation was at stake!

Amanda broke stride when she noticed Hugh Wilmer swaggering away from the cafe in his muscle shirt and painted-on blue jeans. Instinctively, Amanda zipped across the street to collar Hugh before he zoomed off in his truck.

Hugh struck a body-builder pose beside his sporty white Chevy truck and flashed Amanda an engaging smile. "Amanda Hazard, right?" He extended his beefy hand and his biceps bulged. "Hugh Wilmer from Pronto. We haven't been formally introduced, but I've seen you around. Vamoosians have said you're a real looker."

His hazel-eyed gaze toured her body in inspection. Amanda assumed she had passed whatever test she had been given, because Huey flashed her a toothy smile.

"Too bad all accountants don't look like you," Hugh purred in what Amanda assumed to be his lady-killer voice.

Personally, Amanda preferred Thorn's baritone growl.

"Little lady, you can get your hands on my . . . tax forms . . . any ole time you please. We'll have to make an appointment to discuss it real soon."

Amanda removed her hand from the big, blond Don Juan's caressing grasp and went straight for the jugular. Being a divorcee who had been on the singles scene for seven years, Amanda had heard all the come-ons the male brain could concoct, none of which had worked worth a damn until Vamoose's knock-em-dead police chief had come along.

"I've heard you were a close friend of Sheila MacAdo's," Amanda said for starters.

Huey's smile faltered. "Close enough, I suppose. Too bad about Sheila."

"Knowing of her intention to raise your rent on the farm ground and her threats to lease it to someone else, I suspect you're glad to have Sheila out of your hair."

Huey's fading smile flipped upside down in the blink of an eye. "With wisecracks like that, you're getting off on the wrong foot with me, Amanda honey."

"Am I?" She batted her baby blues and tossed him a sugar-coated smile. "Sorry, Huey— "

"The name is *Hugh,*" he interrupted.

"In case you haven't heard, there is some speculation about the possibility of Sheila's demise not being as accidental as first reported. The fact that you were seen at MacAdo Farm the same morning has raised some very interesting questions about your relationship with Sheila."

His tanned face puckered as if he were sucking on a sour grapefruit. "What the hell are you trying to say?"

"I'm wondering if Sheila might have pushed you so far that you decided to push back. She wanted to raise your rent— "

"How the hell do you know that?" he crowed.

"Miz MacAdo is my client." That, of course, had nothing whatsoever to do with how Amanda had gleaned the information, but she doubted Huey was quick-minded enough to figure that out. "There was talk of renting the farm ground to Barnstall or Ogelbee. And then, of course, there was the prospect of Sheila threatening to blab to your wife about your sordid fling, just in case you didn't choose to cooperate."

Hugh's chest swelled like a hot air balloon. "Now, you listen to me, honey, you don't know what you're talking about. Sheila and I were never doing the horizontal two-step."

"No? The Cotton-Eyed Joe then?"

The sarcastic question earned Amanda a snarl and muffled curse. Luckily, she was not the kind of woman who was easily intimidated.

"*P-lease*, Huey, spare me the lies. Everybody around Vamoose knows what was going on with you and Sheila, even if the news hasn't reached your wife in Pronto. Fortunately for you, your wife appears to worship the ground you levitate over. As is usually the case, wives are the last to know their hubbies are screwing around.

"Now that we have that cleared up," Amanda continued, "what time did you arrive at the MacAdo home? Was it before or after Alvin Priddle and Royce Shirley stopped by?"

Hugh stuck out his square chin and glared down at Amanda. "I wasn't there at all and you can't prove otherwise."

"Sis Hix saw you from her kitchen window, so don't waste my time, Huey."

"Quit calling me Huey!" he trumpeted.

"I'll quit calling you Huey when you quit lying through your pearly white teeth. Tell me the truth," she demanded.

His inflated chest collapsed as he propped himself against the side of his truck. "All right, damn it, I was there that morning, but Sheila and I didn't do anything."

"What time?"

"Shortly after ten o'clock. I needed to get this business about next year's rent straightened out. Sheila was insisting on cash rent for the MacAdo farm ground and I wanted to crop rent the property like I always did."

"But Sheila wanted more than a third of the crop since the wheat market is down," Amanda speculated.

"Yes, she did. Sheila was trying to suck as much money out of me as she could get. Hell, I have to deal with plunging grain markets, soaring fuel and fertilizer costs, and weather disasters. But then, Sheila never understood farming, even though she was raised in the country. All she cared about was how much ready cash she had in her bank account."

"So she threatened to lease the land out from under you if you didn't meet her demands?"

Hugh nodded his blond head. "That was Sheila through and through. She could twist your arm a dozen different directions when she intended to have her own way. I wanted to— " He slammed his mouth shut and jerked open the pickup door. "I've got work to do and I don't have time for your prying questions." He got into the truck and revved his engine. "And for your information, I didn't give Sheila a shove when she started throwing her weight around."

That's what they all said, Amanda mused as she watched Hugh Wilmer take off. Somebody around Vamoose was lying and Amanda was bound and determined to find out who— just as soon as she got Thorn's field work done and helped him move his cattle herd to greener pastures.

On that thought, Amanda dodged traffic to return to her Toyota. She glanced through the office window to see Jenny Long working industriously on the tax files.

Amanda should have hired a secretary and housekeeper months ago, she decided as she drove over Whatsit River Bridge. Now she could devote more time to her true calling in life— the investigation of murders that dear, overworked Officer Thorn considered unavoidable accidents.

Nine

Amanda was busy making the rounds on the Allis-Chalmers tractor, humming along with Vince Gill's new country hit, and mentally reviewing the crime scene at MacAdo Farm. She systematically walked herself through Lula's house, scanning the recliner where Sheila's coffee cup sat on the end table beside the phone . . .

Frowning, Amanda negotiated a corner in the field and listened to the machinery clattering behind the tractor. Dust fogged the Allis like a brown cloud as Amanda turned into the wind.

The phone . . . Amanda remembered Lula telling her that Sheila had received a call before Lula left to run errands. Who the devil had called Sheila? Amanda wondered. Could it have been whoever had arrived to give Sheila the fatal shove?

Glancing at her watch, Amanda decided to take an early lunch break and buzz by Miz MacAdo's farm. Considering what Amanda had learned about Sheila and her lazy tendencies, it could well be that the automatic dial function on the phone could provide a clue as to whom the victim called most often. Slothful as Sheila was reported to be, she wouldn't have wanted to waste time dialing or risk breaking a fingernail each time she wanted to speak with her closest associates. Amanda was curious to know who was at the top of Sheila's frequent call list.

Besides that, there was still something about the house and garden that was bothering Amanda. Damned if she could figure out what had looked out of place. And why, Amanda would dearly like to know, had Sheila's billfold been removed from her purse? Had money been taken? Or had the wallet contained incriminating evidence?

"Hey, Ab! Come in!" Clive Barnstall blared over the CB, jostling Amanda from her contemplations.

Static crackled. Amanda turned up the volume to eavesdrop.

"I'm here, Clive. How's the field work going?" Ab came back.

"Hard as cussed rock. How's your ground?"

"The same. I'm pulling up chunks that will take six inches of rain to soften up. My seed bed for the wheat crop will be nothing but clods if we don't get some moisture pretty damned quick. Maybe we should be running the chisel like Thorn's hired hand, instead of plowing."

"I've been plowing this way for years," Clive insisted. "But I must admit that ground Thorn is renting from Amanda Hazard looks a damned sight better than mine."

"Have you heard any more news about the manhunt?" Ab questioned.

"That's what I wanted to tell you. I saw a bunch of squad cars speeding northwest when I drove into town to pick up a new radiator hose. I think the cops finally located the jailbird. Thorn passed me in the ditch with lights flashing and siren screaming. They must be closing in on the escapee. Sure like for them to capture the rascal who stole my truck and swiped my rifle."

So would I, thought Amanda. She was itching to know if Joe Wahkinney had looked Sheila up and pushed her down while he was on the loose. She wondered if Thorn would think to pose a few questions if he had the chance. Probably not. After all, Amanda had failed to convince Thorn that Sheila had run into foul play. Thorn was only accommodating Amanda about this unofficial investigation, to keep the peace.

One of Amanda's bright ideas struck her, and she stamped on the clutch to bring the Allis to a halt beside the gate. Maybe she should grab a couple of burgers from Last Chance Cafe and take them out to Thorn. That way she could casually remind him to question Joe about Sheila.

Thorn would probably kill her for showing up.

Oh well, Amanda thought, scampering toward her car. He had been tempted to strangle her once or thrice, but he always got over it.

Then after a brief conversation with Thorn,

Amanda might still have time to swing by Lula's house and check Sheila's automatic dial on the phone. And with any luck, Amanda could finish this particular field by dark. It would be a productive day. She could kill a whole flock of birds with one stone.

To Nick Thorn's utter disbelief and dismay, he watched the dusty red Toyota fishtail to a halt at each roadblock it encountered, before forging ahead. Nick knew of no one else in the whole damned county who could bluff her way through a pack of cops better than Hazard.

First of all, Hazard's stunning good looks caused the male brain to stall out. Nick well knew that every man with eyes in his head was a sucker for those big baby blues, that shapely body, and natural blond hair— that was presently tinted purple. Secondly, Hazard had become a high profile citizen after solving two murder cases that the local and county police forces had regarded as accidents. With Hazard's impressive credentials, she wound up in places the average Joe couldn't go.

And speaking of Joe . . .

Nick lifted the binoculars to scan the underbrush and thick growth of sand plum trees that camouflaged the creek. As he recalled, this had been one of Joe Wahkinney's favorite fishing holes. Nick had been here a few times with Joe during their teenage years. Lord, the crowd they ran with put away so much beer on those all-night fishing trips that they could have drowned a creek full of catfish . . .

A shadow skipped along the row of trees and Nick focused on the fugitive. "Damned fool," he muttered under his breath. "You were due for parole in four months, Joe. What was your rush? The prison food was good and you had two hundred channels on TV to my lousy seven."

Nick picked up the loud speaker and then set it back down when the Toyota halted beside him. "Hazard, what the hell do you think you're doing?" he grumbled at her.

Blinding Thorn with her hundred-watt smile, Amanda unfolded herself from the seat. She dangled a brown paper sack in his face. "I brought lunch."

Nick scowled at Amanda and her grease-soaked sack. "Bullshit."

Amanda frowned pensively at the sack in hand. "No, high-cholesterol burgers and fries."

Nick expelled an audible sigh and snatched away the carry-out lunch. "What are you trying to pull now, Hazard? And don't give me any baloney about delivering lunch. How'd you get through the road blocks and outer check point stations?"

"I lied my way through, so shoot me."

His dark brows furrowed. "Don't tempt me."

"Thorn, I think you should question Joe about Sheila's death, first chance you get," she said without preamble. "Sheila's billfold is missing from her purse. I had Lula check on it yesterday."

His onyx eyes widened in surprise as he glanced back at the undergrowth that lined the spring-fed creek.

Amanda stared into the distance. "Is that where he is?"

"Yep." Nick bit into his hamburger and then munched on some fries.

Not bad, he decided. The food hit the spot. Nick scooped up the loud speaker. "Hey, Joe, my girlfriend— "

"God, Thorn, you don't have to broadcast it!" Amanda groaned.

"— brought out some burgers and fries from Last Chance Cafe. Sit tight, will you? I'm going to bring one down to our old fishing hole. I'm coming in unarmed."

"Damn it to hell, Thorn," Amanda grumbled, watching him unfasten his holster and lay it on the hood of his black-and-white. "You can't go down there."

"Why not? You barrelled your way through here, didn't you? I thought I might as well give your bold tactics a try. I've had about enough of these goose-chases. I happen to be on my vacation, and I'd like to salvage what I can of it."

"But, Thorn— " Amanda took three steps toward him and found herself swarmed by patrolmen.

Frustrated, Amanda watched Thorn amble through the knee-high bluestem grass like a

Sunday fisherman— with burgers and fries for bait. Mother was not going to be pleased if Thorn got himself shot and couldn't attend the Hazard Labor Day picnic.

"I think you better leave, ma'am," Officer Webb advised. "We don't need a hysterical female on our hands if things get rough."

Amanda shook herself loose from the deputy's grasp and adjusted her Bad Hair Day hat. "I do not get hysterical," she informed him. "I happen to be amazingly well adjusted and emotionally stable. And furthermore, I am not leaving until I'm sure Thorn is all right. He happens to be my boyfriend, you know."

"Yeah, I know. We heard the announcement loud and clear."

Amanda held her breath when Thorn disappeared into the thicket. After two minutes had elapsed, without gunshots echoing across the pasture, Amanda half collapsed against the squad car and waited . . . and waited some more.

Nick halted beside the creek where a small campfire had burned to ashes. The bones of a rabbit indicated Joe Wahkinney had used the rifle he swiped from Clive Barnstall to hunt game for his previous night's supper.

One thing you could count on when dealing with former farm-boy fugitives was their ability to fend for themselves. Joe had been on the run, but he hadn't gone hungry.

Making himself at home, Nick sank down on the grassy knoll and pulled his unfinished hamburger from the sack. "Do you want a sandwich or not, Joe?"

No answer.

"Helluva mess you've gotten yoursclf into." Nick bit into the chiliburger, then dug into the greasy sack. "Well damn, my girlfriend forgot to bring catsup for the fries. That probably won't bother you, though. As I recall, you always liked your fries straight."

There was a quiet rustle of underbrush, but Nick didn't glance behind him. He simply kept on talking.

"I've got another chiliburger and a cheeseburger with the works. Which one do you want?"

After a long silence, Nick heard footsteps behind him. He held up the chiliburger. "Is this still your favorite?"

Looking haggard and unkempt, Joe Wahkinney set the stolen rifle aside and accepted the burger. He sank down beside Nick and stretched his long legs out in front of him.

"Damn Sheila MacAdo," Joe muttered before he bit into the burger.

Nick darted a glance at the man whose rusty-colored hair tumbled over his hollow eyes. Nick didn't like the sound of Joe's comment.

"Yeah, I know, she set you up nice and pretty,

didn't she? Then she yanked your inheritance right out from under you while you were locked away."

"I tried to tell Dad that Sheila was poison," Joe grumbled bitterly. "But he was so flattered by her attention that he wouldn't listen. Hell, she was about my age. Dad had no business marrying her. And when Dad died, I lost my cool. I couldn't believe she had sweet-talked him into changing his will. How could he have done that?"

Nick finished off his sandwich and popped a few fries. "I always wondered if Sheila talked Floyd into making the changes while he was on medication after his first stroke."

"Probably. And she was the one who brought it on my dad to begin with. She was chasing after every stray man who dropped by the cafe."

"I hated like hell to haul you in after you pulled that gun on Sheila and took off with the cash," Nick said with a sigh. "But that was a dumb move, Joe. You played right into Sheila's manipulative hands and she played it for all it was worth."

Joe nodded his tousled head. "Hell, I know that now. At the time I was so damned mad I could barely see straight, and I sure couldn't think straight. I had just buried Dad and Sheila was already flirting with her next patsy. If you had heard her goading remarks about changing the will and cutting me out, you might have pulled a gun on her, too."

"Probably would have," Nick quickly agreed. "I tried to talk her out of pressing charges and so did Lula. We knew it was only grief and frustration that had gotten the best of you. But despite the circumstances Sheila still had a case against you."

"Yeah, and Sheila probably gave the judge and prosecuting attorney a few enticements to make the charges stick. Sheila was something else— a man's worst nightmare."

Nick turned to stare directly at Joe. "Did you go to see Sheila after you escaped?"

Joe's hand, which was wrapped around a half eaten chiliburger, stalled in midair.

"Come on, Joe, level with me. I guess you know Sheila bit the big bullet. You've been talking about her in the past tense."

"Can't say that I shed any tears over her passing," he said, staring across the shimmering creek.

"But you knew before I told you, didn't you?" Nick murmured perceptively. "Wanna tell me what happened?"

Joe sprawled back on the ground and released an enormous sigh. "It probably won't make any difference after I'm hauled back to prison, but at least you'll know the truth." Joe took another bite of the sandwich and swallowed. "After I hot-wired Clive's old truck, I drove over to MacAdo Farm."

Nick inwardly grimaced. If Joe had lost his temper again, after being sent to jail by Sheila's crafty manipulation, he might have craved revenge. Much as Nick hated to admit it, Hazard might have been right about the not-so-accidental accident.

"Where was Sheila when you arrived?" Nick questioned pointblank.

"Dead in the melon patch," Joe reported. "It looked as if she had fallen off her ladder, but I figured everybody in Vamoose would blame me for it if I didn't hightail it out of there—pronto."

"So you took her billfold and the cash to tide you over," Nick presumed.

Joe nodded somberly and then polished off the chiliburger. "She had fifty bucks in cash." He laughed resentfully. "I figured she owed me at least that much for the hell I've been through the past few years."

"So where's the billfold? Did you ditch it?"

Joe glanced up suddenly. "I didn't take her wallet, only the cash."

Nick tried not to look startled, but he couldn't think of one good reason why Joe would lie about a small detail like that. According to Hazard, the billfold was missing. But how could Joe have lifted the cash from the *missing* wallet if Sheila was already dead when he arrived?

God, he dreaded giving this information to Hazard. She'd go wild with speculations. It indicated that something fishy was going on around Vamoose, and Nick would have to admit Hazard might be right. The thought made him inwardly flinch. Being a few mental steps behind Hazard was hard on the male ego.

Nick looped his arms around his bent knees. "This is going to sound like a crazy question, but did you happen to notice any footprints in the garden while you were there?"

"Footprints?" Joe repeated as he munched on the last French fry. "I didn't bother to look. All I saw was Sheila in her short-shorts and the tabby cat curled up on her rump."

"What about the garden rake?"

Joe frowned. "Nope, don't recall seeing any rake lying around. But then, I was in a bit of a rush."

Damn, Nick thought to himself. How did Hazard pick up on minor points the way she did? Sometimes he swore that woman thought and lived on a higher intellectual plane than he inhabited. It was galling to know she could spot clues at a glance while he continued to overlook them.

Joe picked up a twig and tossed it into the creek, watching glumly as it drifted downstream. "Now what are we gonna do, Nick? I'm going stir-crazy in the pen. When I noticed the loose screw on the air-conditioning vent I decided to give it a shot. It was a long crawl through some tight squeezes. But hell, it was good to be on the outside again, just to see if there was still life out here. It's hard on a farm boy who's used to having his own space to be cooped up in a cell."

"You blew your parole, Joe," Nick reminded him.

"Well, if Sheila hadn't stolen my inheritance I might have gotten a decent lawyer the first time around. Maybe I wouldn't have been there in the first place. I told that slack-suit lawyer to check on the new will and Dad's medication, but he didn't waste his time on what he decided was a done deal. The judicial system is crooked, if you ask me."

"Hazard would readily agree with you," Nick mumbled.

"Who's Hazard?"

"My girlfriend."

Joe perked up. "Oh yeah? I'd like to meet her if I ever get out again."

Nick decided, right there and then, that he was going to speak up loudly and clearly now— to compensate for not speaking up back then. Joe hadn't gotten a fair shake. Nick had just come back to Vamoose, after serving in the Oklahoma City Police Department and watching his former girlfriend take a fatal bullet. Joe had been caught in the backlash of one of the worst months of Nick's life.

"Tell you what, Joe. If you give yourself up, I'll get you a good lawyer and see to it that the sheriff reopens your case. He owes me for agreeing to give up my vacation time to track you down."

"You'd do that for me? Why?"

Nick stared down at the shaded creek and thought how fiercely protective and devoted Hazard was to her clients. She would stick her neck out for them— literally. She had done it several times. Nick couldn't help but admire that noble quality. He'd grown a little too callous and indifferent after years on the city police force. He'd seen too many things that he wished he could forget, but couldn't. But his beat was Vamoose now. It wasn't just a job, it was his hometown.

"Why, Nick?" Joe repeated curiously.

Nick climbed to his feet, dusted off his trousers, and outstretched a helping hand. "Hell, Joe, don't make me get all mushy and sentimental here. I want to help you because I feel like it. You're not one of those hard-core losers. And like we've always said around Vamoose, that's what neighbors are for— helping each other out."

Smiling tiredly, Joe reached up to accept Nick's hand. "Sorry I ruined your vacation."

"That's okay." Nick strolled up the creek bank and crossed the pasture, with Joe ambling at his side. "One good thing has come of this. Hazard got a taste of tractor driving. For a city slicker she's not too bad. Of course, her first few rounds in the field were a disaster."

"Big-time skips? Long corners?" Joe asked with a chuckle.

Nick nodded his raven head. "She's making progress, though. It should only take me an hour to clean up her mess, rather than three hours. You'll probably get to meet Hazard sooner than you think. I doubt the sheriff's department managed to shoo her off."

Joe squinted into the sunlight. "That must be her in the blue jeans." He quickly appraised the shapeliest silhouette in the crowd. "Nice body—curves in all the right places."

Nick swallowed down his smile. "Don't make the mistake of telling Hazard that," he advised. "She insists on being known and appreciated for her brains."

"That wasn't Sheila's main concern," Joe muttered.

"No," Nick agreed. "And we all know where it got *her.*"

Amanda sagged with relief when she saw Thorn and the lanky fugitive strolling across the pasture. To her surprise, Thorn paused in front of her and then turned back to introduce Joe.

"Hazard, this is Joe Wahkinney."

He stuck out a long arm and nodded his rust-colored head in polite greeting. "Thanks for the burger, Hazard. It hit the spot."

"My pleasure, Joe."

When the patrolmen closed in, Nick waved them back. "Joe is going to ride in with me. We have a few things to iron out. You boys can take a hike."

The sheriff looked skeptical.

"It's okay. Joe only wanted a hometown hamburger and a little vacation." Nick stared pointedly at the sheriff. "I can identify with that."

When Joe put himself in the backseat of Thorn's squad car and leisurely sprawled out, the patrolmen ambled off. Joe stuck his head out the window when the sheriff walked by.

"Tell Clive Barnstall his rifle shoots wide to the left, or at least it used to. I adjusted the sight. As for his truck, he needed to change the filters and the oil. I did it for him. He should be taking better care of that old truck if he expects it to last another hundred thousand miles. When it comes to repairs, Clive is still as tight as he was when I worked for him in the summers during high school."

"Well?" Amanda whispered aside to Thorn. "Did you ask Joe about the billfold?"

"We'll discuss it tomorrow."

"But— "

Nick pivoted to flash Amanda a silencing frown. "I've got to do some fancy talking to get Joe off the hook for something he got provoked into doing. And for your information, Joe didn't have anything to do with Sheila's fall."

"Or so I'm sure he says," Amanda smirked.

Obsidian eyes bore down on Hazard. "When

Joe left the MacAdo place Sheila was already dead. He took some money, but not the billfold."

The comment got Amanda's complete attention just as Nick predicted. Tossing out that kind of bait always put the bloodhound in Hazard on full alert.

"Somebody must have doubled back to check for incriminating evidence," she mused aloud.

"Whatever the case, Joe had nothing to do with it. You can scratch him off your list of suspects."

Amanda beamed with obvious delight. "So you're admitting my theory of murder might be right?"

Nick cringed at that "I told you so" look that Hazard wore so well. "Let's just say I'm considering the possibility," he hedged. "Now climb back on the Allis and finish the field work while I do what I can for Joe. It may take me awhile."

"I'll have supper waiting."

"Sorry, Hazard, I can't make it. It will take most of the evening to get things squared away with Joe."

When Nick drove off with the manhunt brigade behind him, Amanda glanced down at her watch.

There was no time to stop by Lula MacAdo's home until after work. But before the day was out, Amanda promised to take another look around the MacAdo house and garden.

As for Joe Wahkinney, Amanda wasn't totally

convinced that he was innocent. She wasn't going to scratch anybody's name off the list until she had gathered all the facts. Joe could be taking advantage of Nick's friendship to get him out of all the hot water he was in.

Ten

Amanda stood on Lula MacAdo's front porch, leaning heavily on the doorbell—to no avail. The elderly widow didn't respond, though her Ford LTD was sitting in the driveway beside an unfamiliar midsize green Buick. Concern tripped down Amanda's spine. She kept wondering if the same person who had given Sheila a shove had returned to finish Lula off.

The unsettling thought prompted Amanda to jiggle the doorknob. "Yoo-hoo, Miz MacAdo!" Amanda yodeled.

When Amanda gave the knob a twist she found the door unlocked and immediately burst inside. The sound of muffled voices and footsteps drew Amanda's frown.

"Yo! Is anyone home?" she trumpeted at the top of her lungs.

"Who's there?"

"It's Amanda Hazard."

Amanda's shoulders slumped in relief when she heard the door creak at the far end of the hall. Lula appeared in her oversized blouse and slacks, apparently unharmed.

"Sorry, sugar, we were down in the basement, looking at all the canned goods entered for this year's fair." Lula turned to call Amanda's attention to the immaculately attired young woman who stood behind her. "Have you met my grandniece, Doralee Muchmore?"

So this was the only living beneficiary of the MacAdo estate. Hmmm, very interesting. Had Amanda arrived before Doralee could give Lula a fatal shove down the basement steps? Amanda was going to have to keep her eyes on Doralee.

Amanda carefully appraised the slightly overweight, plain-looking female who sold Tupperware, interior designs, and Jane-Ann Cosmetics. Doralee was living proof that stylish clothes and a heavy coat of makeup could do wonders for unmemorable looks.

"It's nice to meet you, Doralee," Amanda greeted her cordially.

Doralee surveyed Amanda with the trained, experienced eye of a cosmetologist. "You're Aunt Lula's accountant."

"Yes, I am."

Amanda stepped forward, wiping her dirty hand on her jeans. When she offered to shake hands, Doralee stared at the black smears— ground-in residue from the tractor steering wheel— and chipped fingernails and frowned in distaste. Hesitantly, she lifted a creamy hand that boasted shiny red acrylic fingernails.

"I usually don't look like this," Amanda was compelled to explain. "I've been driving a tractor for Nick Thorn while he's busy with the manhunt."

Doralee smiled slightly. "Oh."

It immediately struck Amanda that personality wasn't one of Doralee's stronger attributes. The woman wasn't a sparkling conversationalist, either. How odd that Doralee's profession involved door-to-door sales. It was a wonder she could sell anybody anything. But then, maybe Doralee was much better at one-on-one encounters.

"Doralee just came by to see how I was managing after . . ." Lula inhaled a deep breath. "Well, you know."

Amanda slid the immaculately adorned blonde a discreet glance, wondering if paying respects was Doralee's only motive for dropping by.

"I better be on my way, Aunt Lula." Doralee grabbed her oversized purse by the strap and situated it over her shoulder. "I have a new client who wants a makeover. Sis Hix is trying my line of Jane-Ann Cosmetics."

Good for Sis, Amanda silently applauded. Now that Amanda's new housekeeper had escaped the confines of her trailer home, she wanted to improve her image and boost her self-esteem. Considering what Doralee had done with herself, Amanda was eager to see what improvements the cosmetician could make with Sis . . .

The thought prompted another idea. "Doralee, I'd like to have a demonstration of your cosmetics at your earliest convenience," Amanda requested.

Doralee dug into her monstrous purse to retrieve her appointment book. Lifting her index finger, she swished through the pages with practiced efficiency. "I could do you tomorrow at about 4:30."

Amanda had told Thorn she would help him move his cattle on Saturday. If all went well, Amanda could zip home to shower before Doralee arrived. She could pose a few questions and then race off to the Happy Homemaker ice cream social.

"Four-thirty will be fine, Doralee," she confirmed.

After receiving directions to Amanda's home, Doralee trooped off to keep her appointment with Sis Hix.

"Would you like something to drink, Amanda?" Lula questioned. "Field work probably made you thirsty."

"Sounds good, Miz MacAdo."

When Lula headed toward the kitchen Amanda made a beeline for the telephone. In two shakes she had punched the first button on the automatic dial.

"Hello?"

"Is this the Smith residence?" Amanda quietly questioned the woman on the other end of the line.

"No, this is the Wilmer residence."

"Sorry, wrong number."

Amanda darted a glance toward the kitchen,

hearing the rattle of ice cubes. She punched the second button and heard Royce Shirley's voice on his answering machine. Amanda managed to push the third button, but all she got was a busy signal. Just before Lula returned to the living room, Amanda put down the phone.

"Here you are, sugar. Freshly squeezed lemonade."

Amanda took a refreshing sip. "Mmm, frozen lemonade can't hold a candle to a drink made the old-fashioned way, can it? And store-bought cookies shouldn't even be classified as cookies," she hinted.

"I just happen to have some freshly baked chocolate chip cookies. Would you like some, sugar?"

"My favorite!" Amanda enthused. "I'd love some."

When Lula returned to the kitchen, Amanda made another grab for the phone and punched the fourth button. A low, sexy male voice responded and Amanda blinked in surprise. Who the hell was this?

"I also have some oatmeal cookies left over from yesterday," Lula called out. "I'll bring some of those, too."

Amanda set the receiver in its cradle when Lula veered around the corner.

"There you go. This should tide you over until supper."

Would it ever! There were enough cookies neatly arranged on the platter to feed several hungry field hands. Amanda plucked up two cookies and savored every chew.

"Miz MacAdo, you are an absolute marvel. Nobody cooks as well as you do."

Lula beamed with pride. "I have years of practice to my credit."

After wolfing down several cookies, Amanda strode to the kitchen to return the plate. The tabby cat sat on its window-sill throne, surveying the outside world. Because of the excessive afternoon heat, Lula had closed the window, making it impossible for the cat to come and go as he pleased.

That now-familiar sensation assaulted Amanda when she set foot in the kitchen, alerting her that there was some minute but important detail she had overlooked. She wished she could figure out what the hell it was. The nagging feeling was driving her crazy!

Setting the plate aside, Amanda felt herself oddly drawn to the window. Absently, she stroked the plump tomcat and stared at the garden where watermelons ripened on the vine and tomatoes hung like Christmas tree ornaments.

"Harry Ogelbee stopped by yesterday on his way to the field and offered to repair my picket fence when he gets caught up on his work," Lula said as she walked up behind Amanda. "I think he's trying to get into my good graces so I'll rent the farm to him. He doesn't have as much ground since you inherited the Jolly property and rented it out to Nick Thorn."

The comment made Amanda uneasy. Harry, Ab, and Clive had all rented part of the Jolly ground before Amanda had been named beneficiary by her generous client. All three men had depended on the profit they made from the wheat crops and now the land was unavailable to them. Just how desperate could those displaced farmers be?

"Oh, I forgot to thank you for finding Sheila's billfold," Lula said, offhand.

Amanda pivoted to study Lula's wrinkled features. "You found it?"

Lula blinked. "I thought you must have found it. It was back in her purse and the credit cards were still there, too. The cash was gone though." Lula sighed heavily as she ambled over to return the extra cookies to their proper place. "This week has been a dazed blur to me. Either that or old age is finally catching up with me. I just assumed you found the billfold and returned it after we had discussed it."

Lula glanced over her shoulder and frowned. "You were the one who asked me about the wallet, weren't you? Maybe it was somebody else. I can't seem to recall who said and did what this week."

"It was me," Amanda reassured her. "Would you mind if I looked at it? I don't want to alarm you, but I'm oddly curious about why Sheila's billfold turned up missing and then reappeared."

Lula shook her fuzzy gray head. "There has simply been too much going on, what with the funeral, next week's fair, and plans for tomorrow's ice cream social. I feel as though I've been running around in circles. I volunteered to bring three pineapple upside down cakes to go along with Roxanne Wilmer's cherry cheese-cakes at the ice cream social. She offered to do all the baking, but I didn't want to lay all the responsibility on her."

When Lula waddled down the hall to Sheila's room, Amanda pounced on the phone. She punched the fifth button and heard Alvin Priddle's slow drawl. She hung up on him without a word.

Amanda tried the third button again and heard Mrs. Ogelbee's soft-spoken voice. Good grief, why did the Ogelbees rate as one of Sheila's top five? And who the devil was the man with the sexy voice? Thorn had the sexiest voice in Vamoose, so who was running a close second?

"Here you go, sugar."

Lula presented Amanda with the expensive leather billfold. Sure enough, there was no cash to be found. Thorn had informed Amanda that Joe Wahkinney had taken what money he could get while he was on the run, but who had swiped the wallet and then replaced it?

Amanda glanced out the window, watching the dust from Doralee's car roll across the field.

Refocusing on the wallet, Amanda flipped through the driver's license and credit cards to find one empty slot. "Do you have any idea what might have been in this plastic folder?"

Lula tilted her head back to peer through her bifocals. "Can't say that I do."

Amanda made a closer inspection. There seemed to be a blue tint to the empty folder, rather than the residue of ink that usually stuck to the inside. She deduced that a photograph rather than a printed card had been removed. Hmmm, a photograph of whom? It made her wonder.

Amanda returned the billfold to Lula. "We may never know what was there."

Lula set the wallet on the end table. Tears misted her eyes. "It's all my fault," she burst out.

Amanda wrapped her arm around Lula's shaking shoulders, giving her a comforting hug. "You simply cannot blame yourself, Miz MacAdo. Sometimes things happen that we can't predict or prevent."

"I keep telling myself that," she said with a sniffle. "But— "

"Why don't you grab your purse and let's buzz over to my place. I'll throw something together for dinner."

"Well— "

Amanda refused to let Lula decline the invitation. Lula needed a distraction. She marched over to retrieve Lula's purse from the mantel and handed it to her.

"After I feed my critters, I'll cook us up something and we can watch an old movie on TV."

Lula tucked her purse under her arm and smiled indulgently. "I've got a better idea, sugar.

Why don't you feed your critters while *I* rustle up something for supper."

Although Lula was much too kind to say so, Amanda had the inescapable feeling the widow had heard that Amanda was culinarily challenged. But things were going to change after Amanda won blue ribbons at the Vamoose and Pronto Country Fair. Then maybe she would get a little respect around here.

"Ready, Hazard?" Nick questioned.

Amanda gave a nod and clamped hold of the arm rest in Thorn's 4x4 black pickup. Shifting into gear, Thorn sped over the terrace to herd the cattle he planned to relocate on the pastures northwest of Vamoose.

Since Thorn wasn't a morning person, Amanda kept conversation to a minimum. She decided to give him an hour's grace period before she started firing questions about Joe Wahkinney's incarceration. She also wanted to tell him about the wallet that had been returned to its proper place. But Thorn was in his farmer/stockman mode and Amanda knew the timing wasn't right.

"I tried to got these stupid sons-a-bitches to come into the corral before you got here," Nick grumbled as the truck launched over another terrace ridge. "They stood there and looked at the wide open gate and then made a run for the farthest corner of the pasture. I was ready to shoot them all."

"I don't think you could eat that many steaks before freezer burn sets in," Amanda replied placidly.

Thorn cut her a hard glance. "I'm not in the best of moods, Hazard, and I refuse to be amused."

"Oh really? I hadn't noticed." Amanda braced her free hand against the dashboard when Thorn stomped on the brake.

"Get out and see if you can get these walking steaks to trot along the fence row while I gather the cattle by the pond."

"Yes, sir." Amanda opened the door and stepped out to give Thorn the snappy salute his barked command demanded.

When he grumbled sourly and drove off, Amanda pivoted to assess the situation. Limousin, Simmentol, and Salers cows were grubbing grass into the ground while one Hereford cow stood at a distance, staring into space. It didn't take Amanda long to realize the Hereford was in charge of the calf nursery for the day. There were twenty of the cutest critters Amanda had ever seen lounging in the grass, under the Hereford's watchful brown eyes.

Amanda clapped her hands and shouted the order to put the cow convoy in motion. Thousands of pounds of beef on the hoof simply raised their heads and stared at her. Amanda squared her shoulders and stalked straight toward the nearest cow. To her smug satisfaction the big coward bellowed and took off in a trot, prompting the others to follow after her.

Things progressed without a hitch until the other half of the herd that Thorn was moving with his pickup came romping over the pond dam like a thundering horde. Amanda felt instant panic when the cattle in front of her doubled back at a dead run. There was nowhere to go except up the six-strand barbwire fence and into the bar ditch. She could hear the pounding of hooves and Thorn's loud curses as he gunned the truck and shot across the pasture to cut off the herd.

One of the charging cows rammed a frightened calf broadside, sending it somersaulting in the grass and bawling for its mother. The newborn scrambled to its feet and bolted away from the stampede— and went right through the fence, nicking itself on the barbwire.

Amanda, who was now standing in the ditch, made a wild grab when the terrified calf raced past her. She came up with nothing but tail and found herself jerked forward. The calf bawled as if it had been stabbed, kicked wildly, and tore off like a speeding bullet. Amanda groaned and grabbed her injured elbow, noting the hoof imprint on her upper arm. It hurt like hell.

The foul curses that flooded the cab of Thorn's truck did not bear repeating. Mother would have had a fit if she had been there. Of course, Mother had never tried to drive a cattle herd that had the collective I.Q. of a T-bone steak, either. It was enough to make a saint swear.

"Stay where you are, Hazard," Thorn yelled. "I'll come around through the gate and pick you up. If we don't stop that runaway calf it will keep going until it drops dead."

Amanda shook the sting out of her arm and plowed her way through the tall Johnsongrass. Thorn's truck, looking like a bumblebee with its hay fork protruding from its bed, buzzed across the pasture at a speed nowhere near reasonable or prudent.

While the cattle herd trotted off in all directions, Thorn hopped out of his truck to swing open the gate. Quick as a blink, he was behind the wheel, pausing just long enough to shut the gate behind him. In a cloud of dust and a fog of curses, Thorn roared down the road to pick up Amanda.

"You drive," he ordered as he reached behind the seat to retrieve the lariat.

Amanda pulled herself into the truck and gaped at Thorn. "What are you planning to do?"

"Lasso that dumb calf, of course. What the hell do you think I'm planning to do? Impress you with rope tricks?" Nick gestured toward the road ahead of them. "Step on it, Hazard."

Amanda mashed on the clutch and shifted into first gear.

"I said step on it, damn it!"

Amanda gritted her teeth and slammed into second gear. "When we're finished here, Dr.

Jekyll, we really need to sit down and discuss the Mr. Hyde personality you assume when you're working with cattle."

Nick bared his teeth and glared daggers. "Just shut up and drive, damn it."

Amanda shifted into third and held her tongue, which wasn't easy. Thorn's rotten disposition was spoiling her mood. She kept reminding herself how charming and appealing Thorn could be— except when roundups weren't going according to his expectations.

"Now pull over as close to the calf as you can get without running over it," Nick instructed.

"At thirty miles an hour? What if the calf tries to cut across the road?"

"Then you'll have a freezer full of hamburger, with my compliments." When Hazard looked skeptical, Nick growled at her, "Just do it, damn it!"

To Amanda's amazement, Thorn thrust his head and shoulders out the window of the speeding truck and swung the loop of the lariat.

"Yeah, right, Thorn, like that's going to work— "

Amanda swallowed her skeptical remark when Thorn hurled the lariat and was astonished to see the loop settle over the calf's head. It bellowed for its mother. Thorn gave a firm yank to tighten the rope and the calf flipped onto its back.

"Stop the truck, Hazard!"

Amanda stamped down with both feet— one on the clutch and the other on the brake. The

truck skidded sideways in the gravel, and before
it ground to a complete halt, Thorn bounded
out to restrain the calf. As if he were in a steer
wrestling contest at a rodeo, he dashed toward
the bawling calf and wrapped its hind legs in
rope before it could regain its feet.

Amanda sat there with her jaw sagging.
Thorn had accomplished what she had considered to be an impossible feat. The man didn't
need a horse to rope off of. All he needed was
somebody to drive his truck for him. Amazing!
He had even lassoed the calf on the first try.
Amanda was impressed!

"Damn it, Hazard, don't just sit there like a
slug. Help me load this calf in the back of the
truck."

Amanda shook herself out of her awestruck
trance and scurried through the ditch. "Pretty
fancy ropework, Thorn," she complimented, po-
sitioning herself at the calf's head. She had been
at its heels earlier and expected to have a colorful bruise as a souvenir.

Nick glanced up to meet those baby blues and
couldn't help but grin at Hazard's expression.
It took a lot to impress a woman like her. Nick
had the satisfied feeling he had done just that
with one toss of his lasso. Her smile eased his
black mood considerably.

"Thanks, Hazard. On three. One, two, three."

With a heave-ho, they hoisted the wriggling
calf off the ground and carried it to the bed of
the truck. Once Nick had dallied the trailing

end of the rope around the hay fork, he hopped up beside the calf.

"Drive back to the corral and we'll unload the calf."

Amanda climbed behind the wheel and sped off.

"Hey! Slow down! I had breakfast already. I don't want to eat dust back here!" Nick yelled at her.

A wry smile quirked Amanda's lips as she glanced in the rearview mirror to see the fog of dirt hovering around Thorn. She really must be losing it, she decided. Seeing Thorn in his faded blue jeans, tattered work shirt, his hair ruffled by the wind, appealed to everything female. He looked rugged, rough and tumble— like a renegade from the Old West. Thorn was her kind of man, no doubt about it.

Dreamily, Amanda drove back to the corral, asking herself if a man in an expensive three piece business suit would ever appeal to her again. Probably not . . .

"Well, I'll be damned . . ." came the astounded voice from the bed of the truck.

Amanda discarded her wandering thoughts and eased down on the brake. To her disbelief— and obviously Thorn's, too— the entire cattle herd was standing in the corral, leisurely as you please. Some of them were slurping water from the tank beside the barn while others rubbed against fence posts. After all the trouble— not to mention the considerable cursing Thorn had gone to—the cattle had rounded *themselves* up.

While Amanda circled around to close the gate, Thorn backed up the truck to free the run-away calf. Amanda shook her head and sighed as she watched Thorn stare at his herd with pride and satisfaction. Not thirty minutes ago he was ready to kill them all.

Since Thorn's disposition had sweetened considerably, Amanda decided to ask a few of the questions that hovered on the tip of her tongue.

"Thorn, you never did tell me what happened with Joe. And exactly what was it that convinced you that he had nothing to do with Sheila's death?"

Nick breathed an audible sigh and turned back toward the truck. He had promised to fill Amanda in on the details so he supposed he should be grateful she had held her tongue as long as she had. It must have been some sort of record.

"I persuaded the sheriff to reopen the investigation from six years ago."

When Thorn motioned Amanda back into the truck, she quickly complied. "You didn't believe Joe was guilty of holding Sheila at gunpoint and stealing the cash from the cafe?"

"Yes and no."

"I love it when you're so definite, Thorn."

Nick laid a brawny arm over the back of the seat and backed toward the stock trailer that was sitting beside the corral. "Yes, Joe did lose his cool with his young stepmother, but he was goaded into it. I think Sheila might have pulled a fast one to ensure Floyd changed his will so she could inherit everything. All Joe had for representation in court was a fly-by-night attorney who was only drawing wages. He didn't ask the right questions in court or check into Joe's accusations about the altered will and the circumstances surrounding the incident at the cafe. Needless to say, the attorney is no longer practicing law. Although there isn't much of the Wahkinney inheritance left since Sheila squandered it, I'd like to now clear Joe's name."

"But you don't believe Joe finished Sheila off in order to appease his personal vendetta against her? The man has motive galore, you know. If I were Joe, I might have been tempted to give Sheila a shove myself."

Nick eased up to the stock trailer and stamped down on the emergency brake. "Joe said Sheila was sprawled in the melon patch when he arrived. He went inside to take the cash from her wallet. I believe that's all he did."

"Why? Because he's an old friend of yours? How do you know Joe is telling the truth?"

"Because he was always a miserable liar." Nick hopped from the truck to attach the trailer to the hitch on the rear bumper. "Joe's eyes always dart from side to side when he tries to lie."

"Maybe he got better at lying while doing his stint in jail," Amanda suggested.

"Doubt it." Nick slid onto the seat, released

the brake, and wheeled toward the loading chute. "Joe said he took the cash and replaced the billfold in Sheila's purse."

"He put it back in her purse?" Amanda repeated. "I think you should know that Lula just recently found that wallet. She thought I was the one who recovered it and returned it to its proper place."

Nick blinked, bemused. "You mean the missing billfold is back where it belongs?"

Amanda nodded her lavender-tinted head. "I saw it myself last night when I stopped by Lula's. There was a photo missing from the plastic folder. I would love to know whose picture conveniently disappeared. I have the unshakable feeling that whoever pushed Sheila off the ladder must have returned to swipe what might have been incriminating evidence."

While Nick and Amanda loaded cattle in the stock trailer, Amanda tried to establish the sequence of events that might have taken place the morning of Sheila's fatal fall. But it was difficult to concentrate with cattle bawling and Thorn cursing up a storm when the livestock didn't cooperate.

Finally, Amanda gave up her attempt at analytical investigation and simply filled in as Thorn's hired hand.

Perhaps Doralee Muchmore could provide information while she was giving Amanda a facial. After all, Doralee had a lot to gain from her cousin's demise. Amanda also knew that Doralee

hadn't spilled any tears over Sheila's death. If
she had, Doralee's thick mascara would have
been dripping down her face like Tammy Faye
Bakker's.

Eleven

Amanda hopped into the shower lickety-split. After helping Thorn round up, separate, and shuttle cattle to the pastures, she was running late. Doralee Muchmore was due to arrive in thirty minutes.

Amanda stuck her head under the spray of water to clear the dust from her brain and pondered what Thorn had told her about Joe Wahkinney. The billfold that disappeared and appeared had Amanda stumped. If Joe had taken the cash from Sheila's purse and then replaced it, who had come along to swipe it? And why? What incriminating photograph had been removed? Damned if Amanda could figure it out.

There were several suspects seen arriving and departing from MacAdo Farm. All of them insisted Sheila was alive when they left— all except Joe, the jailbird. Now, Amanda had to determine if Joe was the one who was lying or if he was the only truthful individual in the bunch.

With no time to spare Amanda scurried from the shower and shrugged on her Western shirt and blue jeans. She had just piled her wet, grape-colored hair atop her head when the doorbell rang.

Looking calmly composed and impeccably dressed, Doralee Muchmore surged through the door at Amanda's invitation. "Shall we get started?"

So much for small talk, thought Amanda. The slightly plump, bottle-blonde didn't do chitchat. Either that or she had the personality of a potted plant. Amanda suspected the latter was the case.

"I suggest we work at the kitchen table." With those words, Doralee hiked off with her cosmetic case in hand.

While Doralee picked out liquid and powder makeup, moisturizer, mascara, and several shades of blush, Amanda parked herself in the chair.

"Since Sheila's unfortunate fall, I'm sure Miz MacAdo looks to you for compassion and support," Amanda said casually.

Tilting Amanda's face upward, Doralee poured a glob of makeup into her hand and applied the first thick coat. "My great aunt is a woman of strong constitution. I'm sure she'll bounce back from her recent loss, the same way she has recovered from previous ones."

Doralee's tone was so bland that Amanda wondered if the woman experienced any emotion whatsoever. According to Velma, Doralee had her heart ripped out of her chest when Sheila stole the love of her life. Doralee seemed to have turned to ice after the ordeal— or at the very least, cold-blooded.

Cold-blooded enough to give her female rival a shove and become the beneficiary of the MacAdo inheritance?

"Do you recall what time you arrived at Mac-Ado Farm the morning Sheila died?" Amanda blurted out.

Doralee's hand stalled on Amanda's cheeks. "Who said I was there?"

Amanda didn't answer the question. Instead she fired another one. "Did you and Sheila have words that morning?"

Doralee vigorously rubbed the makeup across Amanda's cheeks and down her jaw. The brisk movements were the only outward indication that Doralee had reacted to the question. Her face was still a carefully coated mask of indifference.

"Sheila and I always had words." Doralee plucked up a compact of powdered makeup two shades darker than Amanda's skin tone. "It's hardly a secret that she and I didn't get along. The fact is that I went by the farm to drop off my entries for the fair. I canned some fruit and vegetables."

Amanda recalled seeing the jars on the windowsill, alongside the watermelon preserves. "Was Lula at the house when you were there?"

Doralee nodded slightly as she patted powder on every square inch of Amanda's face. "Aunt Lula was buzzing around, preparing to leave for town. Sheila was planted in her recliner, fussing about the TV reception and flinging her usual snide remarks at me."

"For instance—?" Amanda slammed her mouth shut when a puff of powder settled on her lips.

"Sheila wanted to know when I planned to lose the extra weight that I try to conceal by wearing an overblouse. And then she—" Doralee halted abruptly, gathered her composure, and reached for the red-rose blush.

"And then?" Amanda prompted.

Doralee inhaled a fortifying breath and brushed a heavy coat of rouge on Amanda's cheekbones. "And then she goaded me about Alvin. Said I'd never have a chance with him, because he was still sniffing around her after all these years. . . . Close your eyes."

Amanda sat very still while Doralee applied a thick coat of eyeliner. "Sheila must have been hell to deal with."

"Hell and then some," Doralee confirmed in her insipid tone of voice. "She was always poking fun at everyone, even Alvin who came running every time she crooked her finger. If he knew all the awful things Sheila said about him he would have given up on her years ago. I don't know what Alvin ever saw in her besides a shapely body. She had the charm of a black widow spider."

"Did you leave the house before Lula did?"

Doralee's experienced hand faltered over Amanda's left eyelid. "Yes."

Amanda wished she could open her eyes to scrutinize Doralee's expression. She wondered if

Doralee was as bad a liar as Thorn believed Joe Wahkinney to be.

"So you weren't there when Sheila propped up the ladder to climb onto the roof."

"No."

"Did you see anyone driving toward the farm when you left?"

"Blast it," Doralee muttered when the liquid eyeliner left splatters all the way to Amanda's eyebrow. Grabbing a tissue, she rubbed the spot clean, taking off the top layer of skin with it. "Why are you asking all these questions? What difference does it make who was where and when? Sheila is gone for good. That's all that matters, isn't it?"

Aware of the betraying crackle in Doralee's voice, Amanda pressed a little harder. "You saw Alvin coming to the house that day, didn't you?"

"Keep your eyes shut," Doralee ordered. "I need to apply mascara to the top side of your lashes."

"Doralee?"

"What!"

"Were you upset when you spotted Alvin's pickup, knowing the hateful comments Sheila had made to you about him?"

"Of course, I was upset," she confirmed, more emphatically than usual.

Amanda quickly reminded herself that Royce Shirley had arrived before Alvin. That suggested Doralee had not told her everything.

"Sheila ridiculed Alvin behind his back and

then preyed on his weakness for her," Doralee rushed on. "She always took advantage of him and every other man in her life. Alvin was entirely too kind to her. That was his problem from the beginning. Alvin was *too* nice. Just look what Sheila made of the poor man. Now he's a borderline alcoholic and she's to blame for it!"

Amanda winced when Doralee's voice hit a shrieking pitch. It seemed there was one topic that could ruffle Doralee's well-groomed feathers. Her sentiments for Alvin were as obvious as the wart on the end of one's nose. Doralee was still fiercely protective of her one and only love— a man driven to drink by a heartless vamp.

Had Doralee doubled back after the flood of males stormed Sheila's door? Had she taken advantage of a perfect opportunity and shoved Sheila into the melon patch? Not only could Doralee have satisfied her long-held grudge but she could also have sealed her financial security. Now she was Lula MacAdo's only surviving heir.

"Open your eyes so I can finish the mascara," Doralee instructed, her voice returning to its normal pitch.

Amanda regarded the woman who hovered over her, remembering her own frustration when Jenny Long had made a bold play for Thorn's affection. Despite Doralee's seemingly calm facade, there were scads of emotions simmering inside her: hatred for her cousin, unrequited love for Alvin Priddle, and smoldering resentment, to name only a few.

Yes, Amanda decided. Doralee had motive aplenty and opportunity galore. She could have returned to the farm to give Sheila a shove and wish her a hearty good riddance.

"Doralee, do you happen to know if Sheila carried a photograph of Alvin in her wallet?"

Doralee blinked and jerked upright. "What kind of stupid question is that? And what does that have to do with anything?"

"Just answer the question, please," Amanda requested in a noncombatant tone.

Her chin elevated in defiance. "I'm sure I wouldn't know."

Amanda wasn't sure about that at all.

"Hold still unless you want wings on your eyebrows." Doralee took pencil in hand and tilted Amanda's head back to an uncomfortable angle. "The total cost of the Jane-Ann Cosmetic kit is $99.95. You can pay in installments like Sis Hix, if you like, or you can purchase items separately. But you should know that the entire kit is more economical."

Amanda had the feeling Doralee had answered all the questions she intended to answer on the subject of her departed cousin.

The cosmetician was now all business.

"I'd like to see the results before I make a decision on whether I want to switch to Jane-Ann Cosmetics."

Doralee dug into her oversize purse and placed her business card on the table. "You can call me if you want to order the kit."

In a flurry of efficiency, Doralee returned the tools of her trade to the cosmetic case. "That will be twenty dollars, please."

Amanda scooted off her chair to retrieve her billfold. When she pivoted around Doralee was lingering in the doorway, looking her phlegmatic, professional self.

Amanda handed over a twenty dollar bill. "Thank you for the demonstration, Doralee."

"You're welcome."

When Doralee surged off, Amanda headed for the bathroom mirror to inspect the results. The reflection peering back at her caused Amanda to retreat two steps. Gawd, she looked like a second-rate hooker with that makeup caked on her face. And worse, the dark shade didn't match her complexion . . .

"Good Lord, Hazard!" came a masculine croak from the hallway.

Amanda wheeled around to see Thorn, decked out in his Western finery, staring at her as if she were a freak from the circus.

"Why the hell did you let Doralee smear that crap on your face? You look like a damned clown."

"I'll have you know this crap cost me twenty bucks."

"You wasted your money, Hazard." Nick propped himself against the doorjamb and grinned while Amanda tried to scrape the thick layers off her face. "You weren't angling for information by any chance, were you?"

"Of course, I was." She glared at his amused reflection in the mirror.

"Did you get your twenty dollar's worth?"

"No." Amanda wiped off as much goo as time would allow. "Thorn, who in Vamoose or Pronto has a voice almost as sexy as yours?" she asked out of the blue.

Nick did a double take. "I have a sexy voice?"

"You darn well know you do."

He smiled rakishly. "Is that what first attracted you to me?"

"No, it was the way you filled out your cop uniform . . . and don't give me that predatory male grin, either. We don't have time to fool around. We have to attend the Happy Homemaker ice cream social."

"Who are you planning to interrogate next?" he asked as he followed Amanda into her bedroom.

"The man with the sexy voice who is listed on Sheila's automatic phone dial."

Nick barked a laugh. "Hazard, your investigative techniques border on the preposterous. I still think you're making too much out of this missing billfold and garden rake business. You said yourself that Lula has been in a tizzy since the accident. She might have removed Sheila's wallet and not even remembered doing it. I've been thinking . . ."

Nick forgot what he had been thinking when Hazard unbuttoned her shirt to change into a more fashionable blouse. Boy, was she ever stacked, and his view from the bedroom door was far more appetizing than visions of home-made ice cream swimming in hot fudge syrup.

When Amanda peeled off her shirt she heard Thorn's throaty purr of masculine appreciation. Her hands stalled in midair.

Nick swaggered toward her—all eyes and a suggestive smile. "We could be fashionably late to the ice cream social. You know how I love spontaneity."

"You said I looked like a clown with grape-colored hair," Amanda reminded him.

With a flair of cavalier devilment, Nick hooked his arm around her waist and lifted her clean off the floor. "I'll close my eyes, Hazard."

Amanda chalked up her instantaneous reaction to Thorn to the awestruck fascination she had experienced that afternoon. Watching him in action, whether policing the streets or ranching, always got to her. The man had so much seductive charm that it practically oozed from his pores. When he looked down at her with those dark, bedroom eyes, Amanda always felt her resolve give way like nuclear meltdown. She definitely had a thing for Vamoose's irresistible chief of police.

Thorn was going to get makeup smeared all over his face if he wasn't careful.

But apparently he didn't care . . . and suddenly Amanda didn't either.

* * *

"Wipe that disgusting smile off your face," Amanda muttered as she and Thorn walked through the parking lot toward the park pavilion. "You look like the proverbial cat that feasted on a canary."

"I've been well fed," he purred, waggling his dark brows.

Amanda elbowed him in the ribs in reprisal. "I think you should interrogate the suspects tonight— casually, of course."

"I'm on vacation and you're doing a splendid job without my help. Besides, there is no official investigation. Aside from a missing wallet that wasn't missing at all and a misplaced garden rake, we have nothing but your suspicious speculations. Can't we just relax and enjoy ourselves for the night?"

Amanda heaved an audible sigh. Thorn still wasn't convinced that he should take her suspicions seriously. He was recuperating from an intensive manhunt and his attempt to see true but belated justice served in Joe Wahkinney's behalf. It was up to Amanda to gather the kind of facts Thorn's brain could relate to.

"Ah-ha, there you two are at last," Velma Hertzog trumpeted when she glanced up from her styrofoam bowl of ice cream topped with hot fudge, whipped cream, and pecans. "You missed Miz MacAdo's welcoming speech."

"Sorry, we were detained by unavoidable circumstances," Thorn replied.

Velma's fake-lashed eyes zeroed in on him before darting to Amanda. Her full face crinkled in a sagacious smile. "Police business, huh? I'll just bet it was."

Amanda knew the gossipy beautician had a pretty good idea what Amanda and Thorn had been doing. It would probably be all over Vamoose by the time the ice cream social wound down.

"I heard you caught your fugitive. Anybody I know?" Velma pried.

"The sheriff's department isn't releasing the name yet," Thorn hedged. "But Vamoosians never really had cause for alarm."

When Velma's head lifted abruptly, Amanda followed her gaze. Hugh and Roxanne Wilmer were making the rounds with all the pomp and pageantry of visiting dignitaries— at least Huey was. He was dressed in his painted-on jeans and sleeveless chambray shirt that displayed his bulging biceps to their best advantage. His shoulder-length blond hair had been shampooed and blown dry. And he had perfected the swagger into what could have been a country-western dance step. The Viking-god cowboy flashed his dazzling smile at every female in the pavilion— except at Amanda. She was obviously on his shit list.

Roxanne Wilmer was unable to keep up with her husband's long, gliding gait. She remained a step behind him, eclipsed by his muscular physique and masculine beauty.

"Hugh has recovered quickly enough," Velma

murmured aside. "I wonder who his next conquest is going to be . . ."

Velma's voice trailed off when Hugh flung Jenny Long an engaging smile. When his left eyelid dropped into a wink, Amanda inwardly groaned. Jenny had just turned over a new leaf and had vowed to improve her image. She didn't need this egotistical loser chasing after her.

When Thorn was dragged off by neighboring farmers who wanted to discuss the lack of rain and field conditions, Amanda kept her gaze trained on Huey. She had never trusted lady-killers.

The thought put Amanda on red alert. Under the pretense of standing in line for a bowl of homemade ice cream, she kept surveillance on Hugh Wilmer. He made the rounds, pausing to chitchat with every female under forty. His wife stood still in his shadow, adding a comment here and there when Hugh permitted her to get a word in edgewise.

On the far side of the pavilion, occupying a table— alone— Alvin Priddle sat with his head bowed over a bowl of ice cream. He looked as if he would have preferred a beer float.

Doralee Muchmore also sat alone at the adjacent table. Now that Sheila was conveniently out of the way, Amanda wondered when Doralee would work up enough nerve to make her move. Doralee kept casting discreet glances at Alvin, but he didn't seem to notice. Maybe Amanda should put Vamoose's matchmaking beautician

to work reuniting first loves. It would keep
Velma focused on a new crusade— and take the
heat off Amanda and Thorn. They needed no
extra heat. They created their own easily
enough, Amanda reminded herself with a secre-
tive smile.

With a dish of ice cream and slice of cherry
cheesecake in hand, Amanda aimed herself toward Royce Shirley. The minute she sat down
beside him, he scooped up his bowl, glared
lightning bolts at her, and made a quick exit.

Amanda silently hurled choice words at his
departing back. It was a good thing Mother
couldn't read Amanda's mind at the moment.
She would have threatened to wash her daughter's mouth out with soap.

Everyone in the pavilion saw Royce give
Amanda the cold shoulder. Make that the *frost-
bitten* shoulder, she amended.

"Well, what's Royce's problem, I wonder?"
Velma levered herself onto the bench beside
Amanda and spooned into her second helping
of ice cream that was swimming with butter-
scotch topping.

Amanda shrugged noncommittally.

"Would you look at Hugh," Velma muttered.
"He's worked his way around the pavilion to corner Jenny Long. He's probably planning to ask
her out while his wife is being detained by Mrs.
Ogelbee. I swear, Roxanne doesn't have a clue
what's going on with her two timing husband.
It must be true that love is blind and stupid."

With extreme satisfaction, Amanda watched Jenny give her dark head a negative shake and walk away. Huey had been shot down. Served him right, the unfaithful jerk.

Jenny parked herself at the table with Amanda and Velma. "Do I have STUPID printed on my forehead or something?" she huffed.

"Certainly not, hon," Velma reassured her. "But you know Hugh is never going to change his ways. As long as there are women on this planet he'll be on the make. And besides that, you look especially appealing in this classy new wardrobe of yours."

Velma glanced back at Hugh Wilmer and frowned pensively. "Say, wasn't Hugh the man rumored to have been fooling around with Sally Marie Taylor a couple of years ago? I heard she was planning to leave her husband for Hugh. That was before she accidentally overdosed on that high-powered medication she took for her migraines. She took them while she had been drinking, didn't she?"

Amanda's investigative nose flared to life.

"I do believe that's the way the story went." Jenny glanced toward the playground equipment to check on her young son who was swinging with a slew of youngsters. "I was living in the city at the time, but I recall my parents mentioning that Sally Marie had been tipping vodka bottles regularly and tried to take medication at the same time."

Lady-killer . . . the words rang in Amanda's ears. First Sally Marie and then Sheila. It sounded as if Huey's lovers had been conveniently disposed of when they began to cause him trouble.

Velma finished off her ice cream and popped a fresh stick of gum in her mouth. "Any woman with a brain in her head knows Hugh isn't going to leave his wife for anybody, no matter how crazy he is about her."

"Why not?" Amanda asked.

Jenny snickered and Velma cracked her gum. "Hon, Roxanne is the one who's got all the cash. She may be as plain as a brown paper sack, but she's an only child and grandchild who inherited oodles of money from both sides of her family. She'll be getting another trust fund when she turns forty. Hugh would have gone bankrupt in farming years ago if Roxanne wasn't financing him. He may run around with the ladies like a stray tomcat but Hugh sure knows which doorstep his food dish sits on."

Amanda pondered Velma's comments as she finished her ice cream. For the life of her, Amanda couldn't decide which suspect had the most to gain from disposing of Sheila.

Hugh couldn't afford to have one of his lovers tattle to his wife. Royce Shirley couldn't afford a lengthy divorce trial and high-priced alimony. Alvin Priddle had been used for years and he might have retaliated in a fit of temper against Sheila.

Then of course, there was Joe Wahkinney who had more than enough reason to do Sheila in. And last but hardly least was Doralee Muchmore who was now sitting on a financial nest egg.

Amanda darted Doralee a discreet glance, noting the cosmetician had finally made her move toward Rag-arm Al. The former baseball star, turned tractor mechanic, lifted his gaze, as if he were seeing Doralee for the first time in a very long time. Al smiled at Doralee and she smiled back. Simultaneously, they reached across the table to clasp each other's hands. Now there was nothing standing between Doralee and the man she adored, except Sheila's bad memory.

Amanda might have been affected by the sentimental scene if she hadn't been so busy trying to decide who to nominate as Most Likely To Commit Murder. Her thoughts evaporated when she heard a deep, drawling voice behind her. *The voice on the phone!*

Twisting around, Amanda came face-to-face with the man whose voice was damned near as sexy as Thorn's.

Twelve

"Who the devil is that?" Amanda asked as she watched the tall, brown-haired cowboy position himself at the end of the serving line.

"Don't you know, hon?" Velma asked. "You do his and his wife's taxes for them."

"I do? I don't think we've ever met," Amanda insisted.

"That's Billy Jane Baxter's husband," Jenny informed her. "Bobby Joe's been back in town about a month, overseeing the last-minute details on the country mansion they're building."

"Bobby Joe had been living at a motel in the city while Billy Jane is on her summer country music tour," Velma elaborated.

Amanda nearly fell off her chair. Sheila had been fooling around with the country music star's hubby? Good Lord, did Sheila have no shame? She had wrecked enough households in her lifetime to make *The Guiness Book of World Records!*

"Are you all right, hon? You look a little peaked? Did you eat your ice cream too fast?"

Amanda shook herself out of her stunned

trance and sized up Bobby Joe Baxter, who was dressed to kill in his expensive western wear. She was certain she knew what Bobby Joe had been doing with his spare time while his famous wife was on the road.

Under the pretense of refilling her ice cream bowl Amanda surged off the bench and made a beeline for Bobby Joe.

"Bobby Joe?" Amanda watched him turn to peer down at her from beneath the brim of a black Stetson with a rattlesnake hatband. "I'm Amanda Hazard, your accountant. We haven't been formally introduced, but I've held several conferences with your wife when she was in town."

Bobby Joe's golden-brown eyes made a thorough sweep of Amanda's feminine assets. "Nice to meet ya, Amanda," he said in his sexy Southern drawl.

"How is Billy Jane's summer tour going?"

Bobby Joe shrugged a broad shoulder. "Okay, I guess. I haven't heard from her this week."

Had the lonely husband looked for affection elsewhere? From what Amanda had learned, Sheila MacAdo had been ever-ready to accommodate the lovelorn— both for the sport and prospective benefits to be gained.

"It must be difficult for you, with Billie Jane on tour so much and the new home in Vamoose to oversee."

"Life can be hectic," Bobby Joe agreed. "We've been trying to get the house finished and furnished before Billie Jane and her band arrive to perform at the Vamoose and Pronto Country Fair."

"I don't suppose you've had the chance to relay the news about Sheila MacAdo to your wife yet." Amanda studied him observantly, noting the deepening brackets around his full, sensuous mouth.

"No, I haven't."

"Too bad about Sheila."

Bobby Joe didn't reply. When his gaze darted toward Royce Shirley, Amanda felt her skin prickle.

"I've heard you've been asking a lot of questions about Sheila's accident."

"You have?"

Bobby Joe nodded, his expression grim. "I advise you to leave well enough alone, Amanda. I went to high school with Sheila. She was a troublemaker from the word go. She called me several times after I came to town, trying to proposition me. I stayed clear of her, just like I did in high school. Now Sheila is gone. I think you should be content with that. Everybody else is."

For sure and certain, Amanda Hazard was not— and never would be.

Before Amanda could drill Bobby Joe full of questions about why his motel phone number was on Sheila's listings, he stepped away to request a double dip of peach ice cream and a slice of Lula MacAdo's pineapple upside down cake.

Grumbling under her breath, Amanda watched

Bobby Joe amble toward Royce Shirley who stood with the cluster of men in the south end of the pavilion. By the time Amanda returned to her table Velma and Jenny were staring accusingly at her.

"Why didn't you tell us you were asking questions about Sheila's so-called accident?" Velma demanded in offended dignity. "I just caught wind of the news from Doralee who was discussing it with Alvin, who mentioned it to Royce. Good gracious! Am I the last one in Vamoose and Pronto to hear the latest gossip?"

"You think somebody bumped Sheila off on purpose?" Jenny questioned, her vivid green eyes wide with surprise. "Is that the reason Royce refused to sit at the same table with you? Because you think he might be guilty?"

"Well, I— "

"Or do you think Alvin did it because Sheila wouldn't come back to him after he fawned all over her all these years?" Jenny demanded.

"Actually, I— "

"I hope you realize you've got Doralee's dander up." Crackle, chomp. "She always defends Alvin when somebody razzes him."

Amanda glanced around the pavilion to see several hostile gazes focused on her. Doralee looked none too happy while she perched protectively beside Rag-arm Al. Royce Shirley, who was smoking like a bonfire, was propped against the metal supporting pole beside Bobby Joe

Baxter. Both men were staring her down through slitted eyes.

Good thing Amanda hadn't entered a popularity contest. She would have taken last place, she thought as she dropped her head and ate her ice cream in silence.

"Who else is on your list of suspects?" Velma wanted to know.

Amanda was saved from the third degree by a youthful squeal, followed by inarticulate jabber. Bubba Jr., dressed in his Sunday best, toddled over to climb onto her lap.

"Now, B.J. you get down from there and let 'Manda eat her ice cream in peace," Bubba sternly ordered his son.

"I'll get him a bowl of his own," Amanda quickly volunteered, escaping Jenny's and Velma's inquisitive gazes. "What flavor do you want, B.J.? Vanilla, chocolate, or peach?"

With B.J.'s stumpy legs clamped around her waist, Amanda strode toward the serving line.

However, Amanda quickly realized she had committed a tactical error by leaving the table. Jenny and Velma scattered, spreading gossip like wildfire. By the time Amanda had retrieved B.J.'s ice cream—a dip of each flavor—Thorn was looming over her like a billowing storm cloud.

"I want a word with you, Hazard," he growled.

"I can't right now, Thorn. I'm entertaining Bubba Jr. He likes me."

Thorn bared his pearly whites. "Bubba Jr. appears to be about the only one around here who does. All your *suspects* have demanded to know if I'm opening an official investigation, and why *you're* in charge of interrogation. And those who aren't suspects want to know why in the hell—"

"Don't swear in front of B.J. He's at an impressionable age."

"So am I, Hazard, and I'm getting the impression that I've been entirely too lenient with you," Thorn fumed. "This was supposed to be a social event, not a police line up!"

Thorn clamped his fingers around Amanda's elbow and towed her toward the Hixes. "Bubba, I need to speak privately with Amanda."

Bubba pried his son loose from Amanda and planted him on the nearest bench. Before the toddler squealed in outrage, Bubba set the dish of ice cream on the table in front of him. B.J. grabbed his plastic spoon and dived in.

"You look very nice this evening," Amanda complimented Sis.

Sis, who had made a visit to the Beauty Boutique and had purchased the Jane-Ann Cosmetic kit, beamed with pride. "Thanks, 'Manda. After we paid the plumber and air conditioning repairman, Bubba insisted I take what was left of my new salary and pamper myself."

"Come on, Hazard," Thorn muttered as he shepherded Amanda out of earshot.

"Before you slide into your aggravating role of male dominance, I think you should know it was Velma and Jenny who were circulating gossip. I was minding my own business."

"You almost never mind your own business," Thorn said with a dark scowl. "You envision yourself as the female version of the Lone Ranger and I wind up being your Tonto, or Batman's Robin, or Roy Roger's Gabby Hayes—"

"I get the point, Thorn."

"Damn it to hell, Hazard," Thorn ranted on. "I'm Vamoose's chief of police! But even though this is my turf and my beat, you're always getting harebrained vibes that launch you into one of your haphazard investigations. And before you're through, I'm usually bombarded by irate Vamoosians who want to know if they've been accused of a crime that I'm still not sure has been committed!"

"You're yelling, Thorn," Amanda calmly pointed out.

"Of course, I'm yelling. I'm mad as hell! I'm supposed to be on the first real vacation I've had in two years. The next thing I know you'll decide the accident Harry Ogelbee had Thursday is somehow related to this supposed case."

"What accident?" Amanda demanded.

Nick cursed himself for opening his big mouth. "Harry was on his way to replace the boards in Miz MacAdo's picket fence when a speeding vehicle whizzed through a blind intersection in a cloud of dust. Harry hit the brakes, skidded on loose gravel, and rolled his truck in the ditch."

"Who was driving the other vehicle?"

"Harry doesn't have a clue. He's got a blinding headache and a concussion from smacking his skull on the side window, plus several bruised ribs. The weeds were so tall in the ditch that they obstructed his view until it was too late. He thinks the vehicle might have been green and that it blended in with the weeds, making it impossible for him to see it until the last second. I don't think anybody was trying to do him in because he's been angling to rent the MacAdo farm ground," he added emphatically.

Nick inhaled an enormous breath, making his chest swell to gigantic proportions. "And now, if you don't mind, Hazard, I would like to get the hell out of here before I have to deal with an unruly crowd that is probably ready for an old-fashioned lynching— yours. I've got endless hours of tractor work ahead of me tomorrow. I'd like to call it an early night."

"Then why don't you go ahead without me and I'll catch a ride with— "

"No." Thorn propelled Amanda toward his truck. "You've stirred up enough trouble for to-night. Tornadoes do less damage around here than you do!"

Amanda resigned herself to the fact that she would not be allowed to socialize and scare up more facts. But she did keep her eyes peeled for green vehicles while Thorn shuffled her through the parking lot.

There were at least a dozen green automobiles

and trucks. Amanda wondered which one of them was responsible for Harry Ogelbee's accident.

Hell and damnation. Amanda wished Thorn hadn't mentioned the accident. It was liable to send her off on another wild goose chase. She'd been on enough of them already, what with trying to collect, sort, and store facts that might be vital to a case Thorn preferred to ignore. But he wouldn't take Amanda's suspicions seriously until clear-cut evidence leaped up and slapped him in the face.

It was up to Amanda to see that it did. Thorn would thank her for it— eventually. . . . She hoped.

When Amanda arrived at her office bright and early Monday morning, Jenny was already seated at her desk, busy as a bumblebee in a bucket of tar. The coffeepot was sputtering and a pan of homemade cinnamon rolls posed an impossible temptation. Amanda wolfed down two before inhaling a breath.

"You left the ice cream social too early," Jenny said as she glanced at her new boss. "A fight broke out in the parking lot and Bubba Hix was the only one big enough and brave enough to break it up."

"Oh?" Amanda swallowed the last delicious morsel of cinnamon roll. "A fight between whom?

"Royce Shirley and Hugh Wilmer."

Amanda poured herself a steaming cup of coffee. "What did they come to blows about?"

Jenny swiveled in her chair. "About who gave Sheila a shove, of course."

"And where was Doralee while this was going on?"

Jenny blinked at the unexpected question. "Gee, I don't know."

"Where was Alvin Priddle?"

"I didn't see him, either. I was too busy watching Royce punch Hugh in the eye and Hugh punch Royce back. They're both sporting shiners. Roxanne Wilmer was beside herself when her husband split his lip and got his perfectly straight teeth loosened. I guess she didn't want her pretty boy roughed up."

Nor did Doralee want Alvin fighting over the memory of a woman who had practically ruined his life.

"From what Velma and I heard, Royce made some wisecrack about Hugh being at Sheila's house the morning of the fatal fall and then doubling back to make Royce and Alvin look suspicious. Hugh threw what was left of Roxanne's home-baked cherry cheesecake in his face and Royce lit into him. Before Bubba could pry them apart they were both covered with glazed cherries and blood. Now all of Vamoose thinks one or the other of them did Sheila in, but won't admit it."

Amanda grimaced. When Thorn got wind of the fisticuffs she would take the blame. News traveled fast over the CB radios. The farmers, while working in their fields, were as bad about spreading gossip as the clientele at the beauty shop and cafe.

Amanda made a mental note *not* to be at the office during the lunch hour. Thorn would probably climb down from his tractor and drive to town to jump down her throat. Maybe Jenny could pacify him with her mouthwatering cinnamon rolls.

As Amanda wheeled toward her desk she saw a green midsize car pull into the parking lot at Last Chance Cafe. She strode to the window to sip her coffee. The same green automobile that had been parked at Lula's a few nights earlier came to a halt. Doralee Muchmore, looking immaculate, as always, stepped out.

Amanda wondered if Doralee was the one who had been flying down the gravel road and caused Harry Ogelbee to roll into the ditch Thursday evening. Doralee, as Amanda recalled, had also been at Lula's house the day the missing wallet turned up.

Hmmm . . . the door-to-door saleswoman had an amazing knack for showing up at the right places at the right times, didn't she?

"How is your uncle Harry Ogelbee feeling after his truck accident?" Amanda questioned.

"Uncle Harry is recovering nicely," Jenny replied. "My aunt brought him home from the hospital yesterday."

"Did Harry ever figure out who was driving the car that he avoided smashing into?"

"No, and my aunt is still fuming because the motorist didn't have the decency to stop and check on him."

Small wonder why the mysterious motorist didn't, Amanda thought, glancing out the window toward Last Chance Cafe. "I'll be back in minute, Jenny."

"What do you want me to do with Velma's tax forms when I finish typing them up? Put them back in the file cabinet?"

"You can drop them off at the beauty shop for Velma to sign after I get back. I'll man the phone while you're gone."

In determined strides, Amanda aimed herself toward Last Chance Cafe. She had a few more bones to pick with Doralee Muchmore. Amanda found Doralee at the counter, ordering two cups of coffee.

"You seem to be exceptionally thirsty this morning," Amanda noted.

Doralee— cool and collected as ever— turned her carefully coiffured head to appraise Amanda's professional business suit. "Yes, I am, as a matter of fact."

"On your way to see Alvin, is my guess."

"And what is that supposed to mean?" Doralee challenged in a guarded tone. "Are you trying to create more trouble than you already have?"

Amanda displayed a bright smile. "No, I was

just speculating on who would actually be drinking the second cup of coffee. I noticed you and Alvin were together at the ice cream social."

Her chin tilted upward. "So?"

Amanda discarded her cordial tone since Doralee wasn't being the least bit receptive. "So, now that Sheila is conveniently out of the way, you can rekindle your old flame with a man who desperately needs rehabilitation and direction in his life."

Doralee's well-schooled expression puckered into a glower. "I suggest you back off and mind your own business, Amanda. If you persist in prodding rattlesnakes, you could get bit."

"Or shoved off a ladder?" Amanda daringly ventured.

"Just leave it alone," Doralee responded with a growl.

"That's what Bobby Joe Baxter said."

"Well, maybe you should follow his good advice before you suffer an unpleasant accident yourself."

On the wings of what sounded suspiciously like a threat, Doralee trooped off with her two cups of coffee.

Amanda glanced around the restaurant to see several pairs of curious eyes watching her. Amanda did the only thing she could do, she smiled pleasantly and followed Doralee out the door.

"Stay away from me, Amanda," Doralee threw over her shoulder. "Anyone seen talking to you automatically becomes another suspect. I don't want you to ruin my reputation in Vamoose. My business and financial success depends on my rapport with my clients."

"I hardly think you need to concern yourself with securing a financial future. You're Lula's only surviving heir. I, being her accountant, know she has amassed a sizable fortune in savings accounts and property."

For a moment, Amanda swore Doralee intended to hurl the steaming cups of coffee at her. Somehow though, the cosmetician managed to restrain herself.

Glaring fireballs, Doralee maneuvered her coffee cups into her green Buick and drove off.

When Doralee disappeared from sight Amanda muttered under her breath. She had the inescapable feeling she was very close to solving this case. She simply needed to sit herself down and ponder the chain of events leading up to Sheila's death. Amanda was going to do exactly that when she caught up on her office work, she promised herself. The pieces of this puzzle were scattered around her head in disarray, but all she had to do was funnel her thoughts and energy to the task. Then maybe this nagging feeling that kept hounding her would finally settle into its proper place. She could only hope!

Resolved to spending the evening in pensive meditation, Amanda walked across the street to her office. At 11:45 Amanda drove home for lunch, hoping to avoid Thorn. Jenny could handle him— figuratively speaking.

Amanda preferred not to be around when Thorn blew up. She couldn't afford a distracting argument. Her head was full of unassimilated facts and information. She didn't need Thorn clogging the workings of her analytical mind right now. That sexy cop caused her brain to short circuit often enough as it was.

Thirteen

The door to Hazard Accounting Office banged against the wall and Nick burst inside, still fuming. He had been simmering since he'd heard the news over the CB that a scuffle had erupted in the parking lot after the ice cream social. Damn that Hazard. When she took it into her blond head to investigate an accident she turned the town upside down and set Vamoosians buzzing like a disturbed bee hive.

"Where the hell is that woman?" he growled at Jenny's silk-clad back.

Jenny swiveled around in her chair to meet Nick's narrowed onyx gaze. "Hi, Nicky. Are you upset about something?"

Upset with *someone* was nearer the mark. "Where the hell is Hazard. I want to give her a good piece of my mind!"

"She went home for lunch today."

She probably realized he would hear about the battle over the CB and come gunning for her. "The big chicken," Nick muttered half under his breath.

Jenny frowned at Nick's inarticulate mumbling. "Pardon?"

"Never mind." Nick inhaled a deep breath and caught wind of Jenny's homemade cinnamon rolls. "Is that what I think it is?"

Jenny smiled proudly. "I practiced making a batch of cinnamon rolls before taking my entry to the fair. Would you like some?"

Would he ever! Nick had skipped breakfast in his haste to climb on the Allis and finish his field work.

For the first time in a month, the meteorologist had given Vamoose County a high probability of rain. Storm clouds were already piling up on the southwest horizon like oversize cotton balls. Nick had granted himself enough time to chew Hazard up and spit her out for inciting the fight, grab a burger for lunch, and then hightail it back to the field. But he decided to forego lunch and devour Jenny's famous, melt-in-your-mouth rolls. If there was one thing Nick missed about Jenny, it was her out-of-this-world cooking.

Too bad Nick had developed this wild attraction to Hazard who couldn't cook a lick.

"Lord, Jen, these are delicious," Nick complimented between succulent bites.

"Well, at least I can do one thing better than Hazard," she said with a rueful smile.

Nick peered down into vivid emerald eyes. "One of these days you'll find the right man for you, Jen," he predicted. "Be particular and patient."

"What a shame that I let the best one slip away when he joined the marines. Amanda is lucky to have you, Nicky. I hope I find someone just like you." Jenny rose from her chair to loop her arms around his neck. Smiling, she pushed up on tiptoe to press a kiss to his sugar-coated lips . . .

And that was when Velma Hertzog lumbered through the door with a batch of tax forms clamped in her stubby fingers. "I signed the forms and brought them back—"

Velma hauled her hefty body to an abrupt halt when she saw Jenny and Thorn. "Ah-oh . . ."

Nick inwardly groaned. He and Hazard had been on solid footing the past few months and now this! If Nick knew one thing for sure about Hazard it was that she was extraordinarily sensitive about loyalty in male-female relationships. Her ex-husband had had an affair right under her unsuspecting nose and she had been the last to know. It had taken Nick months— not to mention considerable effort— to earn Hazard's trust.

If the caretaker of Vamoose's grapevine blabbed her big mouth, Nick would have a battle royal on his hands, trying to convince Hazard that the chaste kiss he'd shared with his ex-girlfriend had no romantic connotations whatsoever.

Jenny did the worst possible thing she could do. She retreated two steps, wearing an expression that looked guilty as sin. Nick expelled a colorful curse.

Accusing eyes, rimmed with thickly coated false eyelashes, bounced from Jenny to Nick. "As I was saying, I just came by to return my signed tax forms so you could send them off to Uncle Sam. Where's Amanda?"

"Out to lunch," Jenny mumbled, refusing to meet Velma's damning stare.

"Well," she said, snapping her gum, "the two of you should be ashamed of yourselves!" Velma threw back her thick shoulders and rested her fists on her hips. "Out of the goodness of her heart, Amanda gave Jenny this job so she could make a fresh new start and put an end to any female rivalry. And this is the thanks she gets?"

Nick tried to interrupt and failed. "Now, Velma, we—"

"And you!" Velma aimed her explosive artillery at Nick and let loose with both barrels. "You're the chief of Vamoose police, the symbol of integrity! It took me months to convince Amanda that the two of you were perfect for each other."

"Velma, it wasn't—" Jenny got nowhere fast.

"For heaven's sake, Jenny. How could you betray your new boss like this?" Snap, chomp, crack came the sound of her gum. "You wanna be Vamoose's next Sheila MacAdo? I'm mad enough to give you a shove, and I'm not even the woman betrayed! The more I think about it the more I think Amanda is right about Sheila getting pushed off her ladder. And if a crime hasn't been committed yet, there might be one soon." Velma glared at the twosome in condemnation. "If I had a pistol I'd blast a few holes in both of you!"

In thumping strides Velma stalked over to slam the tax forms down on Jenny's desk. "Isn't that just like a man— fooling around when a good woman has her back turned."

Velma rounded on Jenny and made a stabbing gesture with her index finger. "And here I've been working on the perfect match for the *new you*, Jenny. I don't know why I wasted my valuable time on a traitor!"

"Velma!" Jenny wailed, to no avail.

Velma stormed out the door and never looked back.

Jenny covered her face with both hands and burst into tears. "I'm sorry, Nicky. I wasn't trying to cause trouble like before!"

Nick patted her shaking shoulders while she continued to cry. "Don't worry about it, Jen. I'll explain to Hazard." Somehow. He hoped.

A rumble of thunder shook the windowpane. Nick glanced toward the threatening sky and scooped up two more cinnamon rolls to tide him over until supper. "I've got to get back to the field. With any luck I'll finish in a couple of hours, just before we get this much-needed rain."

Jenny sniffed and inhaled a steadying breath. "I better get back to work myself. I don't want to look like I've been crying when Amanda comes back from lunch." She sucked in another shaky breath and blurted out. "Oh, Nicky, I'm not sure I can face Amanda, knowing Velma will tell her what she thought she saw!"

"I'll take care of it," Nick reassured her on his way out the door.

Nick paused outside to survey the roiling clouds. He really should make a beeline to Hazard's house and nip the gossip grapevine in the bud before it ripened. But the angry clouds indicated an impending storm, and Nick needed to finish his field work and pull the tractor back to his farm before he was mired in mud. His explanation to Hazard was simply going to have to wait.

Hurriedly, Nick climbed into his black pickup and whizzed off, munching on the cinnamon rolls that had become his lunch.

Amanda wheeled into her driveway, greeted by a grumble of thunder. She wondered if it was actually Thorn cursing at her— all the way from town. He should have arrived at her office by now, eager to chew her up and spit her out, because of the fisticuffs at the social.

Noting that her red jalopy truck was gone, Amanda presumed Sis and B.J. had hurried home to prepare lunch for Bubba. A curious frown knitted Amanda's brow when she noticed

the rectangular package sitting on the corner of
her porch.

A care package from Mother, Amanda predicted. Mother was known to send her children
survival kits from time to time. Amanda grimaced, remembering the last package she had received from Mother. The box had contained
single servings of prunes, raisins, a month's supply of dental floss— Mother had a penchant for
dental hygiene— and articles from the newspa-
per that Mother considered noteworthy.

Amanda scooped up the package. She
frowned again, noting there was no return address. Boxes from Mother always boasted a return address, bordered by flowery designs.

When Pete, the three-legged dog, yelped in
greeting, Amanda wheeled around with her
package balanced on one palm and her house
key in the other. She nearly toppled off the
porch when Pete bounded forward, and to avoid
trouncing on the handicapped dog, Amanda
sidestepped. The heel of her black pump slid
off the side of the concrete porch and she fran-
tically clutched at the supporting beam. To her
dismay, the package tumbled off her hand, collided with the edge of the cement, and cart-
wheeled onto the grass.

B O O M ! ! !

Amanda and Pete howled when the force of
the explosion knocked them backward. Clumps
of grass and dirt showered them.

Amanda collided with the window behind her

and braced herself with whatever means available. Pete let out several shrill whines and headed for cover as fast as three legs would carry him.

In stunned amazement, Amanda stared at the hole in her lawn. Her ears were ringing something fierce. The pungent smell of ammonia and combinations of toxic scents she didn't recognize permeated her senses. Her eyes watered in reaction to the acrid fumes and dust particles that filled the air. For several moments Amanda simply braced her shaking hands against the window frame, staring down at the jagged pieces of glass around her feet, wondering if she would ever be able to hear normally again. She was fairly certain her eardrums had shattered like the window.

When she felt something wet and sticky on her fingertips, she glanced down to see the stream of blood oozing from the side of her left hand which was clamped around broken glass.

Apply first aid. That single thought filtered through her malfunctioning brain.

On wobbly knees, Amanda unlocked the door and negotiated her way into the house, hearing nothing but a hum of silence. After rinsing the deep cut on her hand she retrieved the largest Band-Aid in the medicine cabinet and stuck it over the wound.

Amanda glanced up to note that the world was beginning to tilt on its axis and turn fuzzy around the perimeters. The loud explosion had affected her equilibrium. She had to lie down before she fell down. The shock was beginning to wear off and her body was vibrating like a paint shaker.

A bomb? she thought, dazed. Someone had delivered a bomb? Just because she dared to pose a few questions about Sheila's not-so-accidental death?

Yikes! Somebody had tried to blow her away—or at the very least, scare the living daylights out of her. Who? Which foot that she had stepped on felt threatened enough to kick back?

Get a grip, Hazard told herself as she sprawled on her bed. Amanda practiced deep breathing for a few minutes before she reached out a trembling hand to pluck up the telephone. The only number that hadn't been blown out of her stupefied mind was the one at her office. Amanda punched in the numbers and cursed her quaking forefinger when it slid off its target. With willful determination she began the process again.

Amanda still couldn't hear anything except an amplified buzz in her ears. She couldn't tell for certain if Jenny had answered the phone. Nevertheless, Amanda yelled into the silence— or tried to.

She couldn't even hear the sound of her own voice!

"Amanda?" Jenny strained to interpret the blaring jabber on the other end of the line. It was obvious, she thought, that Velma had marched back to the beauty shop to call Amanda and tattle.

Jenny was beside herself. She was grateful for her new job and proud of her new beginning. Now it had been ruined by a hug and kiss for old time's sake. She had only wanted to let Nick know there were no hard feelings between old friends.

"I'm sorry!" Jenny yelled back. "It was nothing, really it was. It was only a peace-treaty kiss. I think you and Nicky are perfect for each other, too. Please don't fire me—"

Jenny grimaced when Amanda's bugle-like voice came down the line nonstop. After a moment, Jenny calmed down enough to translate part of Amanda's garbled sentences.

"Boom!" Amanda blared for the third time. "Hole in the lawn . . . broken window . . . cut hand . . ."

"My God, Amanda, you shouldn't become self-destructive or try to demolish your own property because of a harmless kiss!"

Jenny hit the panic button when Amanda started screaming her head off again. "Stop yelling and listen to me. The kiss meant nothing. I swear it!"

"Got to get Thorn," Amanda hollered.

Jenny blinked, confused. "Get Thorn? God, you aren't planning to shoot him or something, are you?"

"Almost dead."

"You're planning to shoot him until he's almost dead?" Jenny wailed. "Listen to me, Amanda. I promise it will never happen again— "

"Got to get Thorn!"

Jenny glanced wildly around while Amanda continued to yell. It was clear that Jenny was unable to reason with Amanda. The poor woman was having the queen-mother of conniption fits.

Jenny dropped the receiver in its cradle, switched off the computer, and grabbed her purse. She had to find Nicky and fill him in on the catastrophic chain of events. Maybe between the two of them they could make Amanda understand the situation that Velma had completely misinterpreted.

Frantic, Jenny dashed outside. A blast of cool, moist wind slapped her in the face. Thunder echoed in the distance as she scurried to her car. It would take her almost a half hour to reach the farm where Nicky was working in the field. There was no telling how much damage Amanda could do to herself and her property in that amount of time!

Nick scowled when raindrops splattered on the windshield of his tractor. "Gimme a break here, will you? If you'll just give me time to work the corners, you can send a cloudburst, for all I care. Is fifteen minutes too much to ask?"

Thunder boomed. Nick presumed the answer to his divine request was *no*.

Shoving the tractor into fifth gear, Nick sped diagonally across the field, bouncing over the rough terrain like a rubber ball on concrete. The film of dirt on the windshield mixed with the huge raindrops and dribbled into streams of mud. He couldn't see where the hell he was going.

Switching on the wipers, Nick squinted through the muddy rivulets. He stamped on the clutch and spun the steering wheel before he crashed into his own fence. The heavens had opened and rain pounded down like a waterfall.

Swearing inventively, Nick shifted to third gear and reversed direction. The red clay ground was already becoming slick enough to lose traction, forcing Nick to decrease speed even more.

If he could make it to the gate before the ground became saturated, he could finish the field work before the Allis and the heavy implement bogged down completely. And if he was really lucky, he might be able to dodge a lightning strike.

Sitting in a tractor with metal chisels stuck into the ground was not a good place to be during an electrical storm. And Nick didn't relish the thought of being stuck on the Allis. He preferred getting his sizzling charges with Hazard— if she was still speaking to him.

Nick put the tractor in second gear and muttered under his breath. Damn Velma and her bad timing. That motor mouth of hers could spoil the good thing Nick and Hazard had going. The only snag Nick and Hazard had hit lately centered around her idiotic investigations. Now Nick was probably going to have to defend himself against a crime *he* hadn't committed.

Lightning flashed across the blackened sky and Nick reflexively ducked. Thunder crashed and rain hammered on the windshield like drumming fingertips. To hell with finishing the corners, Nick decided. He was getting out of there before he was fried to a crisp!

He had just maneuvered to the gate when the blinking headlights of an approaching car caught his attention. To his astonishment, Jenny Long pulled up beside the tractor and dashed out into the downpour.

"Nicky!" Jenny called over the roar of the tractor and pounding rain.

The alarmed expression on Jenny's face, and the very fact that she was standing out in the storm filled Nick with apprehension. He shoved down on the throttle and hopped off the tractor in a flash.

"What's the matter, Jen?"

"Velma told Amanda about the two of us!" Jenny blubbered. "Amanda called and yelled at me over the phone. I tried to explain to her but she just kept screaming at me. She said she was going to get you."

Nick swore under his breath. He had spent months coaxing Hazard into unpacking all the emotional baggage she had been lugging around because of her ex-husband. Now the confidence Hazard had graciously bestowed on Nick had been destroyed by a harmless kiss and friendly hug. Damn it to hell.

"I'll take care of it, Jen. You go home and dry off, then go back to the office and get your work done."

"But I feel responsible—"

"I said . . . I'll take care of it. Now go!"

Nick grabbed her by the shoulders and directed her toward her car. After Jenny reluctantly drove off, Nick jockeyed the tractor and machinery through the field gate and parked on the side of the road, leaving barely enough room for traffic to get past the heavy equipment. Dripping wet, he climbed into his pickup and headed for Hazard's house.

Nick dreaded the upcoming encounter. According to Jenny, Hazard had flipped out. He wondered if the innocent until proven guilty theory would apply to this situation. Only time would tell, Nick reminded himself. He would simply face the music and see what tune Hazard was singing.

With windshield wipers flapping, Nick turned onto the road that led to Hazard's house and very nearly suffered the same sort of accident that had rolled Harry Ogelbee's truck in the ditch. A speeding vehicle materialized out of nowhere, camouflaged by the tall weeds and curtain of rain.

Swearing mightily, Nick swerved to the right.

The truck slid in the gravel and Nick stamped on the brake. He cursed the phantom vehicle that made no attempt to slow down in the intersection. Nick couldn't get a make or model, much less a license number before the car— or truck, he couldn't tell which— sped off in the downpour.

When the tires on the passenger side of the truck dropped into the ditch, Nick switched to four-wheel drive. The tires spun on the rain-slickened weeds and the truck fishtailed, half in and half out of the ditch near the blind intersection.

"Damn it, Commissioner Brown," Nick muttered. "Hazard is right. You need to get your butt out here and mow these damned roadsides!"

Nick made a mental note to call the county agency first thing in the morning. The tall weeds were a traffic hazard . . .

And speaking of Hazard . . . Nick inhaled a fortifying breath and navigated down the puddled road. The rain still hadn't let up when he pulled into the driveway. Nick didn't wait for it to, either. What did it matter? He was already dripping wet.

A muddled frown crossed his face when he spotted the hole in the lawn that stood half full of water. He glanced at the porch to see splinters of plastic lodged in the wooden supporting beam. Chunks of broken glass littered the porch.

"Good Lord, Hazard, what did you do?"

With grim determination Nick strode to the

door, finding it unlocked. He stepped into the living room to see more broken glass strewn about on the damp carpet.

"Hazard, where the hell are you?"

No response.

Nick walked into the kitchen to see Hank casually sprawled beside his food dish. Hank stirred, stretched, and ignored the intruder.

"Hazard!" Nick hollered again.

Veering toward the hall, Nick approached the bedroom. He pulled up short when he spied Hazard, lying spread-eagle on the bed. Her grape-colored hair was caked with dirt and grass. Her face was freckled with debris, and there were shallow cuts on her forehead and cheek. His assessing gaze dropped to her left hand, noting the oversize bandage that didn't quite cover the bloody slice that stretched from thumb to wrist. Her eyes were closed and even her eyelids and lashes were speckled with dirt and grass.

"Hazard?" Nick approached the bed, but she didn't stir at the sound of his voice. Nick reached down to give her a nudge. "Hazard, what the hell have you been doing?"

Amanda's eyes popped open and she nearly leaped out of her skin when she found the drenched Nick Thorn towering over her.

"It's about time you got here!" she yelled crossly.

Jenny was right, Nick decided. Hazard was obviously still in the screaming phase of anger.

She was hollering at him as if they were standing on opposite sides of an ocean.

"Calm down, Hazard."

Frustration was eating Amanda alive. She could see Thorn's lips moving, but she couldn't hear a blessed word he said. "Somebody tried to kill me!"

Nick blinked at the blaring sound of Hazard's voice and reassessed her appearance. "Holy hell!"

Nick sank down on the bed beside her and pulled away the Band-Aid to inspect the deep gash that was still oozing blood.

"Good God, Hazard," he croaked. "We need to get you to Dr. Simms— pronto!"

Fourteen

When Nick scooped Amanda up in his arms, she was still lightheaded and her ears were ringing like wind chimes. This was one time that she appreciated male domination. Thorn would ensure she received proper medical attention.

Amanda frowned when Nick strode into the living room and deposited her on the sofa. She watched him pick up the phone that she hadn't heard ring.

"Hello?"

"Thorn, is that you?"

"Yes, Mother."

"My goodness, you're at Amanda's house quite a lot, aren't you?" There was strong disapproval in Mother's voice. "I hope the two of you aren't inviting gossip."

"Mother, I—"

Mother cleared her throat and cut Nick off. "It seems to me that the two of you should consider marriage if you're going to be spending so much time together. But you can hardly do that, because you refuse to meet the family. Goodness gracious, Thorn, have you got some serious mental or physical defect Amanda doesn't want us to know about?"

Nick ignored the insult. "Mother, I'm a little short on time here."

"Well, let me speak to Amanda."

"She's short on time, too." Nick glanced down at his disoriented companion. "Maybe you should call back tonight."

"Maybe you should hand the phone to my daughter!" Mother harumphed. "Last I knew *she* was still ruling the roost over there!"

Nick put a stranglehold on the receiver, pretending it was Mother's neck, and offered the phone to Amanda. She simply stared blankly at him. "It's your mother, Hazard."

"I can't talk on the phone," Amanda yelled, pushing the receiver away. "I can't hear a damned thing, Thorn. The bomb blew holes in my eardrums."

"Bomb?" Nick parroted.

"Bomb?" Mother caterwauled. "Did she say bomb? What bomb? What is going on? Is my daughter all right? Good grief, Thorn. You are the police chief in that po-dunk town. What kind of clown lets that sort of thing happen? Do you let every yahoo in Vamoose— ?"

"I'll call you later, Mother." Nick said in his most authoritative voice. "Your daughter is fine." Sort of. "We have some business to attend at the moment."

Mother was still yammering a hundred miles a minute when Nick hung up the phone and squatted down in front of Amanda. When he started posing questions, Amanda shook her tousled, lavender head and made a stabbing gesture toward the notepad on the coffee table.

"You'll have to communicate with me on paper," she yelled.

Nick hurriedly scooped up pen and paper. *WHAT'S THIS ABOUT A BOMB?*

"There was a package on the porch when I came home for lunch," Amanda hollered, after reading the written question. "I figured it was one of Mother's survival kits she sends every so often. When I picked it up, Pete bounded around the corner of the house and hopped on the porch to greet me." Amanda paused to cover the wound on her hand when it dripped on her skirt and swallowed hard.

GO ON, Nick wrote.

"Don't get your briefs in a bind, Thorn," Amanda growled loudly. "What's left of my brain is malfunctioning. Don't rush me." She inhaled a bracing breath. "Now, where was I? Oh yeah, I remember. Pete and I got tangled up in each other's legs and I nearly stumbled off the porch. I caught myself on the support beam, but the package tumbled onto the ground. Then BOOM ! ! !"

Nick reflexively blinked and shrank away when Hazard flung up her arms in a wild gesture.

WHAT ABOUT THE BROKEN WINDOW? Nick questioned on paper.

"The impact knocked me backward and I must have shattered the glass," Amanda yelled in explanation.

YOU DON'T HAVE TO YELL, HAZARD. I CAN HEAR YOU, EVEN IF YOU CAN'T HEAR ME.

"Sorry, Thorn." Amanda tried to lower her volume, but she had no idea if she had.

She hadn't.

"The explosion sent a blast of dirt and grass into the air and I tried to get away from it. I remember hitting the wall and grabbing hold of whatever I could latch onto to steady myself. I wound up holding broken glass."

WE BETTER GET YOU TO THE DOCTOR. YOU NEED STITCHES.

Amanda nodded agreeably. "Thorn, can I ask you something?"

ANYTHING, HAZARD.

She peered into his handsome bronzed face which registered worry and concern. "If I had been blown to bits, would you have missed me much?"

Amanda became the recipient of a hug that practically squeezed the stuffing out of her. Thorn then proceeded to kiss her breathless. It was a long moment before her pulse rate returned to normal.

DOES THAT ANSWER YOUR QUESTION, HAZARD?

Amanda managed a smile as Thorn picked her up and cuddled her close. He strode through the rain to plant her directly beside him in the truck.

With trouble lights flashing, Nick zoomed off to the hospital to locate Dr. Simms. This was the third time Hazard had required medical attention during one of her unofficial investigations. Nick cursed himself thoroughly for refusing to acknowledge Hazard's finely tuned instincts.

Mother was right, although Nick hated like hell to have to admit it. He was not taking very good care of her precious daughter. Hazard had almost gotten herself blown to kingdom come, because he refused to believe Sheila's death was anything except accidental.

Dr. Simms walked into the emergency room, his high-top Reeboks squeaking on the recently waxed floor. "What kind of trouble has our self-appointed private detective gotten herself into this time?"

Since Hazard still couldn't hear anything, Nick spoke on her behalf. "A bomb blew up in her face and she can't hear anything. She also sliced her hand on a broken window."

Dr. Simms squeaked over to the examination table on which Amanda was perched. After intently inspecting her hand, he called to the nurse.

"I'll give Amanda a tetanus shot, just to be on the safe side. Never know what might have lodged in this gash, what with debris flying every which way."

"Ouch!" Amanda yelped when Dr. Simms stabbed her with the syringe.

"Sorry about that."

"What?"

Dr. Simms waved off her question and reached for another needle to give her a local anesthetic. While he waited for the shot to numb the affected area he checked her ears.

"Hand me the Q-tips," he requested.

The nurse quickly complied.

Dr. Simms removed the debris and inspected both eardrums. "I don't detect any permanent damage, but Amanda is definitely experiencing hearing trauma."

"Well, that's a relief." Nick would never forgive himself if Hazard had suffered permanent injury because he had been too preoccupied and too stubborn to take her suspicions seriously.

"You need to lie down," Dr. Simms ordered Amanda. Gently, he eased her onto the examination table and plucked up the sutures. In a few minutes he had stitched her back together and then levered her into a sitting position.

"There you go. Good as new— almost," he decreed.

"What?"

Dr. Simms patted her compassionately on the shoulder and graced her with a reassuring smile. To Thorn he said, "She's all yours. I'm prescribing a few days of bed rest. If Amanda's hearing hasn't returned by the end of the week, you better bring her in for extensive testing."

"You don't happen to have a straitjacket I could borrow, do you?" Nick questioned, staring pensively at the bedraggled patient. "Hazard isn't known for her ability to lead a sedate life. She has entirely too much energy for that."

"So I've discovered. Last time she was here I thought I'd have to tie her down to keep her overnight." He pivoted to pluck up a plastic bottle and then crammed two tablets in Amanda's mouth. "Give her a dose of these sedatives to make her sleep."

On the wings of Dr. Simms's well-wishes for a speedy recovery, Nick carried Hazard back to his truck. The rain had finally slacked off when he veered into Hazard's driveway. Once Nick had Hazard tucked in bed, he went to pour her a diet Coke.

Nick handed Amanda her favorite beverage and a note. *I'LL BE BACK WITH YOUR SUPPER AFTER I DRIVE THE ALLIS HOME.*

Amanda nodded sleepily. She had the feeling whatever medication Dr. Simms had shoved down her throat was a sleeping potion. She could barely hold her eyes open.

She needed to sift through the facts she had gathered in this case, but the medication was clouding her thoughts. Although procrastination wasn't one of her shortcomings, Amanda decided to follow Scarlett O'Hara's policy of worrying about it tomorrow.

* * *

When the office phone blared, Jenny Long snatched up the receiver. "Hazard Accounting Office. Jenny speaking."

"Jen? Nick."

"Is everything okay?" she asked anxiously.

"No, I'm afraid not. Somebody tried to blow Hazard to smithereens with a packaged bomb."

"Oh, my God!"

"She's resting comfortably now and she hasn't gotten wind of what happened between us at the office," Nick reported. "Hazard was yelling at you because the explosion damaged her hearing."

"Oh, my God!" she repeated.

"I wondered if you would have time to cook something up for supper and bring it by her house. I've got to move my machinery home."

"Sure, Nicky. I'll be glad to. I was just getting ready to leave the office."

"Thanks, Jen. I'll meet you at Hazard's in a couple of hours."

Nick replaced the receiver and rummaged through Hazard's purse to retrieve her house key. He wasn't taking chances on the perpetrator returning while Hazard was unaware. She was too vulnerable at the moment.

Locking all doors and windows behind him, Nick walked off. He paused, frowned thoughtfully, and then switched direction to locate Pete. The three-legged dog was tucked inside the barn, still covered with grass and dirt. There were two nicks on his back— undoubtedly from falling glass. Otherwise, the dog appeared to be healthy enough.

"Come here, Pete," Nick called.

Pete just stared at him. Nick had the inescapable feeling that Hazard's crippled dog couldn't hear any better than she could.

Amanda was nudged awake, finding Jenny Long hovering over her while Thorn was propped against the bedroom doorjamb. Jenny set a tray of steaming food on her lap and handed her a fork.

"Thank you," Amanda yelled appreciatively.

Jenny glanced over her shoulder at Nick. "Did you tell her that she doesn't have to yell?"

"Sure I did, but she can't seem to tell the difference."

"It's a relief to know she wasn't actually screaming at me," Jenny said with a sigh.

"What?" Amanda loudly demanded.

Nick scooped up the notepad and pen. *NOTHING, HAZARD, JUST SMALL TALK. EAT YOUR SUPPER.*

Amanda dived into the delicious fried chicken, mashed potatoes, gravy, and corn-on-the-cob. She decided that after she won blue ribbons at the fair for her green beans and peaches she would establish a name for herself in the other culinary arts. Creamed tuna on toast sim-

ply didn't compare to Jenny's savory meals.
Maybe Amanda would try to become a bit more
domestic and find time to learn to cook now
that she had an assistant at the office and part-
time housekeeper. And next year, perhaps she
would enter a few baked pies in the fair competition rather than a store-bought cake mix.

"Thanks, Jen. Will you be able to take care
of the office for the next few days without Hazard?" Nick asked.

"I'll do what I can." With a wave of farewell,
Jenny went home to feed her son.

When the phone rang Amanda continued to
devour her meal without so much as a blink.
Nick strode over to answer the call.

"Hello?"

"Well? *Now* are you going to tell me what's
going on in that rinky-dink town?" Mother demanded, as only Mother could. "What did that
bomb business have to do with my daughter?"

"She was at the wrong place at the wrong
time," Nick reported. "Amanda has a temporary
hearing loss, is all."

"Hearing loss? My Lord!" Mother yowled.

Nick held the phone away from his ear before
Mother damaged *his* eardrums. "The doctor expects Amanda will be her old self in a few days."

"What doctor? Some quack in Nowhere, Oklahoma? Bring Amanda over here and I'll drive
her to a qualified specialist in the city."

"There's no need," Nick insisted. "Amanda
is receiving excellent medical care. Are there any

messages you want me to relay to your daughter?"

"I called to remind her about the Labor Day picnic next weekend."

"I believe you have mentioned it twice already. In case you haven't heard, your picnic is the same day as the Vamoose and Pronto Country Fair."

"That can't possibly take all day and half the night," Mother sniffed. "Not in that dinky one-horse town."

Nick summoned patience. "We may be running a little late. I'll be working the police booth to raise money for charity. I have to dismantle the booth before we can leave."

"Good grief," Mother groused. "You would think this was the World's Fair!"

"Anything else, Mother?" Nick forced himself to ask.

"Yes. Amanda's brother needs financial consultation. His spendthrift wife can't balance a checkbook to save her simple-minded soul."

Nick had the feeling Mrs. Hazard would be the mother-in-law from hell. "I'm afraid financial advice from Amanda will have to wait until next week."

Mother cleared her throat. "Thorn, are you planning on marrying my daughter or not?"

"When? Tonight? No. She can't hear well enough to repeat the vows."

"Don't be sarcastic, Thorn," Mother huffed. "If there is one thing I detest it's sarcasm."

"I'll bear that in mind, Mother."

"You're doing it again, Thorn."

"Sorry."

"No, you aren't," Mother accused.

Nick smiled to himself. One of these days he was going to come face-to-face with Mother. It would probably be a memorable encounter.

When Amanda tried to climb out of bed to refill her glass, Nick clamped a hand on her shoulder and stuffed her back onto the stack of pillows.

"Gotta run, Mother. I'm waiting on Amanda, hand and foot."

"Well, I should hope so since it's your fault that she— "

"Oops." Nick dropped the receiver, watching it clatter into place, and then snatched the empty glass from Hazard's hand. "Stay put."

"What?"

Nick gestured toward himself then pointed at the empty glass. Amanda nodded in comprehension and watched tentatively as her swarthy male nurse sauntered down the hall. When Thorn returned, barefoot and bare-chested, Amanda arched a surprised but appreciative brow. Thorn set the glass on the end table and handed Amanda a note.

I'D LIKE TO SHOW YOU EXACTLY HOW MUCH I WOULD HAVE MISSED YOU IF YOU HAD BEEN GONE FOR GOOD. ANY COMPLAINTS, HAZARD?

Thorn didn't give Amanda time to reply.

Even though she couldn't hear the sound of her own voice, much less anybody else's, she had no trouble interpreting Thorn's scintillating style of communication. Under Thorn's skillful ministrations, she was starting to feel much better. But then, she had never found fault with the tender loving care Thorn could provide.

After enduring four frustrating days of silence, Amanda finally regained her hearing. During her recuperation she had studied all the information she had collected in the case. Thorn had taken his last few days of vacation from the police force to investigate the incident involving the homemade bomb. Then he set about questioning everyone on Amanda's list of suspects. Thus far, Thorn had come to the same conclusions Amanda had arrived at. Any number of people could have been provoked to retaliate against Amanda, because she had cried murder and pointed several accusing fingers.

Although Amanda had meticulously compiled her notes, listing incidents in chronological order, she had still come up with a big fat nothing. She was, however, leaning heavily toward one suspect in particular— Doralee Muchmore. Doralee had issued a threat the same morning the bomb had been delivered. Doralee definitely had the most to gain when Sheila vamoosed from Vamoose permanently. But then, Royce

Shirley saved himself a considerable sum in court costs and alimony.

Amanda frowned as she reread her notes. Come to think of it, she couldn't completely rule out Alvin Priddle, either. Those silent types often turned out to be deadly and dangerous. Rag-arm Al could have thrown Amanda a curve as well. He was a tractor mechanic who had access to all sorts of electronic devices and chemicals that could be used to build a bomb.

And then, one couldn't overlook the Viking-god cowboy who had come to blows with Royce. Amanda would dearly like to know what that argument was all about. It could be the key to this case.

Sighing in exasperation, Amanda set her notes aside and padded barefoot to the kitchen. The country fair would be held tomorrow. She had a German chocolate cake to bake for the fundraising auction.

According to Thorn, the carnival rides were being set up at the park and the fair board was making its last-minute preparations. Amanda was anxious to see the look on Thorn's face when she strutted away with her prizewinning beans and peaches. Of course, Doralee Muchmore would probably be spitting mad when Amanda won awards in the fruit and vegetable categories.

Mad enough to leave another bomb on Amanda's doorstep?

Amanda retrieved the cake box that sat in alphabetical order on the kitchen shelf. She dumped the ingredients in the bowl and mixed thoroughly, according to directions. While the layer cake was in the oven, Amanda gathered her notes and once again reconstructed the sequence of events that led to finding Sheila sprawled in the melon patch.

Fact Number One: Doralee had arrived to enter her fruits and veggies with the fair board president before Miz MacAdo left for town.

Fact Number Two: Royce Shirley, who had access to several chemicals in his feed store, had supposedly arrived before Sheila made her fatal fall into the garden.

Fact Number Three: Alvin Priddle had made his appearance shortly after Royce left the scene— or so they both said. Amanda could not rule out the possibility that both men were providing alibis for each other.

Fact Number Four: Hugh Wilmer showed up after Alvin left the scene. Or were all the ex-husbands and lovers providing alibis for each other?

Fact Number Five: Joe Wahkinney claimed Sheila had already cracked her melon before he arrived to swipe money from the billfold that was first missing and then later found.

Amanda drummed her fingers on her notes, wondering if Hugh really was the last one to see Sheila alive, or if one of the other suspects had doubled back before Joe Wahkinney arrived.

The only person Amanda could safely say was

innocent of planting a bomb on her porch was Joe. That did not, however, mean he hadn't bumped off Sheila.

It was entirely possible that one of the suspects was afraid he/she might be accused of the crime and had tried to scare Amanda off.

Big mistake. The attack had the reverse effect. Amanda was more determined than ever to solve the mystery. And furthermore, the attack had brought Thorn around to Amanda's way of thinking. The perpetrator had succeeded in provoking Thorn to open an official investigation.

Too bad most of the clues were older than stale bread by now.

When the oven timer buzzed, Amanda smiled gratefully. She was never going to take hearing for granted again. The only advantage to being deaf was missing the overprotective lectures of Mother's phone calls.

The door bell chimed and Amanda called out from the kitchen. "Come in, it's open."

A few seconds later Thorn loomed in the doorway. "Damn it, Hazard, you're supposed to keep your door locked . . . What the hell is that?"

Amanda followed his gaze to the two lopsided cakes in the oven. She obviously hadn't divided the batter equally. One cake had spilled over the edge of the pan and the other one was half full. Oh well, Amanda encouraged herself. A thick layer of icing would conceal her mistake.

"This is my cake for the fundraising auction," she announced.

Nick stifled a groan. Sure as the sun rose, Hazard expected him to bid on her nightmare cake. It would probably cost him a half-day's wage to spare her embarrassment.

Nick discarded his wandering thoughts and concentrated on the matter at hand. "I finished questioning Alvin Priddle and Doralee Muchmore— "

"Separately or together?"

"Separately.

"Learn anything new?" Amanda set her cake pans on the stove and watched in dismay as the centers caved in. She would have to whip up a double batch of icing to cover the sink holes.

"No, I didn't." Nick expelled a frustrated sigh. "They both gave me the same story they gave you. I can't prove either of them doubled back to commit the crime at MacAdo Farm."

"I intend to pose a few more questions at the fair," Amanda announced.

"And I'm hoping to identify the green vehicle— at least I think it was green— that nearly sent me the same way Harry Ogelbee went."

Amanda wheeled around, goggle-eyed. "What? When was this?"

"The day you received your anonymous bomb. I was on my way over here in the rainstorm. The car zipped through the country intersection and I didn't see it until it was almost too late. Lucky thing I have four-wheel drive. I might still be stuck in the ditch."

It had to be Doralee Muchmore, Amanda decided. Doralee had the perfect motive. She drove a green car and carried a long-harbored grudge against Sheila. She also was heir to the MacAdo fortune.

Tomorrow Amanda was going to provoke and prod Doralee until that cool-headed, impassive-faced cosmetician broke down and confessed.

It was going to be a grand day, all the way around, Amanda assured herself confidently. She would impress Thorn with her powers of deduction and walk off with prizewinning fruits and vegetables. Now, if she could salvage her flattened cake and sell it for a high price at the auction she would truly be the Culinary Queen for the day.

That inspiring thought prompted Amanda to give Thorn a zealous hug.

"What was that for, Hazard?"

"Because I felt like it."

Nick backed away, shifting uneasily from one foot to the other. "Um, Hazard, there's something I need to tell you . . ."

Nick stared down into that blinding smile and those twinkling baby blues and decided not to spoil Hazard's good mood. The incident with Jenny in the office could wait. Besides, he had more suspects to question before he set up the police booth for the fair.

"I gotta run, Hazard. I'll see you at the fair."

Amanda turned back to her cake and grabbed the recipe book. She needed to whip up icing as thick as caulking. Damn, becoming a culinary queen was taking more time than Amanda wanted to commit to claiming the title!

Fifteen

Fifteen

Amanda balanced her lopsided German chocolate cake with both hands and closed the door of her Toyota with the sway of her hip. Ah, the day of the Vamoose and Pronto Country Fair had finally arrived.

Amanda glanced around the parking lot, nodding cordially to the excited attendees who filed past her. Children were squealing in anticipation of piling into the carnival rides while their parents viewed the arts and crafts exhibits and canning and baking competition. Future Farmers of America students were grooming their livestock before leading them into the show ring to be judged.

The junior and senior high school students had set up their fundraising activity booths on the far side of the park. There were basketball shooting contests, an archery competition, horseshoes— dozens of activities to entertain young and old alike.

Amanda could hear the bursts of laughter after one of the participants in the egg-tossing contest missed his catch and wound up with yolk splattered across his face. Mmm, this countrified atmosphere was the best dose of medication for whatever ailed you. It also took the edge off Amanda's nerves, knowing Thorn was to be interrogated and put on display at the Hazard Labor Day picnic later that evening.

In high spirits and with great expectations, Amanda aimed herself toward the entry table to donate her cake for a good cause. She'd had to stab a dozen toothpicks into the cake to prevent the top layer from sliding off. But it didn't look all *that* bad, considering. It was the taste that counted, Amanda reassured herself.

Amanda's anticipatory smile faltered when she set her donation in front of Velma Hertzog who was in charge of entries for the cake and pie auction. Velma stared at the pools of icing that formed around the edge of the cake and then cast Amanda a pitying look.

"It was the best I could do," Amanda defended herself as she lifted her injured hand. "I was handicapped."

"It isn't that, hon," Velma said ruefully.

"What's wrong?" Amanda demanded to know.

"They didn't tell you, did they?"

"Who?"

Velma heaved an audible sigh and penned Amanda's name to the entry tag. Her fake lashes fluttered against her full cheeks like monarch butterflies. "I saw Nick and—"

Just then Gertrude Thatcher walked up to enter her strawberry cake. Velma swallowed her words, filled out a new tag, and sent Gertrude on her way.

Velma leaned across the table to convey the confidential information. "I saw Nick and Jenny at your office together— kissing. And you better believe I gave them what-for. Those shameless turncoats. And to think of all you've done for Jenny." Crackle, snap went her gum. "Of course, I haven't breathed a word about this to anybody else."

Amanda felt as if an unseen fist had slammed her stomach against her backbone. Her mouth opened and closed like a damper on a chimney, but no words came out. Amanda was too stunned to speak. She was still standing there dumbfounded when Sis and B.J. Hix arrived to enter a blueberry pie— Thorn's favorite. Amanda was tempted to purchase the pie on the spot and throw it in Thorn's low-down, lying, cheating face!

"Hi, 'Manda, how are you this morning?" Sis greeted her cheerfully.

Amanda nodded mutely and scooped up B.J. who peered up at her with a beaming smile— rimmed with the usual milk mustache. "Fine thanks, Sis. How are you feeling these days?"

"Much better. Now that the air conditioner has been repaired I haven't had so many bouts with morning sickness."

"Mind if I take B.J. to the fishing pond booth to see what prizes he can pull out of the water?"

"If you want to."

B.J. jabbered excitedly, pointing a miniature finger toward the plastic swimming pool that served as a pond. Well, at least Bubba Jr.'s affection was sincere, Amanda comforted herself. Too bad she couldn't say the same for Thorn and Jenny. Damn it, just when you thought you knew somebody and could depend on their loyalty— whomp. They stabbed you in the back.

With B.J. draped on her hip, Amanda threaded through the crowd. She paused momentarily to watch a judge appraise four spotlessly groomed lambs in the show pen. Four anxious teenagers braced their sheep and waited for the judge to thoroughly inspect their animals and select the winners.

Good thing Amanda wasn't asked to judge. She obviously couldn't pick a winner. Damn that Thorn. He was turning out to be just like her ex-husband. The sneaky weasel!

Thirty minutes later, Bubba galumphed over to retrieve his babbling son from Amanda's arms. She surveyed the crowd of Vamoosians who were scattered hither and yon. She was in just the right frame of mind to flush out the culprit who had shoved Sheila off her ladder and left a bomb on Amanda's porch.

Amanda spotted Doralee Muchmore and Rag-arm Al standing in line, waiting to take their turn at throwing softballs at the dunk tank. Amanda made a beeline toward the booth. It made her feel better to see that Thorn was the individual positioned on the collapsible seat above the water tank.

DUNK A COP, the sign read. Amanda, given a preference, would have liked to strangle him.

She was quick to note that Rag-arm Al still retained most of his pitching speed and accuracy from his high school baseball career. His first pitch hit the target dead center. Thorn dropped like a rock, splashing water over the giggling bystanders. Rag-arm Al threw three perfect strikes and Thorn came up looking like the drowned rat he was— to Amanda's everlasting satisfaction. When Alvin turned to accept his prize Teddy bear, Amanda thrust a five dollar bill at him.

"You're on a roll, Alvin. See if you can strike out the side."

While Al fired pitches and Thorn kerplopped in the dunk tank, Amanda rounded on Doralee. "I hear you were the cause of two traffic accidents while you were buzzing around, covering your tracks."

Doralee blinked at the abrupt comment. "I don't have the foggiest idea what you're talking about."

"Don't you?" Amanda smiled cattily. "It was your green car that caused Harry Ogelbee's accident while you were on your way to return Sheila's billfold."

"That is utterly ridiculous," Doralee huffed, her cool facade cracking like bad plaster.

Amanda ignored the denial. "And you are also the one who breezed through the intersection after leaving the homemade bomb on my porch. You ran Officer Thorn off the road that day."

The thick layer of Jane-Ann Cosmetics coating Doralee's face wrinkled like an accordion when she glowered at Amanda. "I was nowhere near your house the day the bomb went off. I was having lunch with Alvin in Pronto."

Amanda bared her teeth. "Prove it, Doralee."

Doralee spun around to tap Alvin on the shoulder. "Alvin, tell Amanda that we had lunch together Wednesday in Pronto."

"We had lunch together Wednesday in Pronto," Al repeated before winding up to throw at the target.

Thorn took another plunge into the tank.

"You're lying," Amanda muttered to Doralee.

Doralee smiled mockingly and threw Amanda's words back in her face. "Think so? *Prove it.*"

Grumbling under her breath Amanda strode off. It seemed Doralee and Al had rehearsed their alibis. Now Amanda was going to have to devise another method of obtaining a confession of guilt. The direct approach hadn't worked worth a damn.

Of course, there was the possibility that Amanda might have made a slight miscalculation. Maybe Doralee really wasn't the one who had zipped around the country, covering tracks after Al and/or she committed the crime . . .

Amanda's frustrated thoughts trailed off when she spotted Huey Wilmer swaggering along beside his wife. Roxanne had prepared her famous cherry pie for the auction. The pie

looked exactly like the ones Amanda's grandmother used to make with the lattice-work crust
on top. Perhaps Roxanne was as plain as butcher
paper but she could make every dessert imagin-
able with her favorite fruit. If Lula MacAdo was
the Watermelon Preserve Queen of Vamoose,
then Roxanne was the Cherry Queen of Pronto,
Amanda thought to herself.

"Out to cause more trouble today, just like you
did at the ice cream social?" Hugh smirked as
he stared down at Amanda from his body-build-
ing pose.

"Wanna cherry pie in your face rather than
cherry cheesecake?" Amanda flung back at him.

Hugh's cocky smile vanished as he loomed
closer, his long blond locks waving in the summer wind. "Watch it, little lady. If you get on
my bad side like Sheila did, I'll—"

"You'll what? Chase me up a ladder and then
push me off of it?" she boldly challenged.

Huey's steely fingers curled, as if measuring
Amanda's throat for a choke necklace. "I'm
starting to feel real bad about the fact that you
didn't manage to blow yourself up with that
bomb this week."

"And I'm kicking myself to Pronto and back
that I arrived too late to actually *see* you shove
Sheila into the melon patch and then rake away
your tracks after you made sure Sheila was gone
for good," Amanda flung right back at him.
"You could be in the slammer right about now,

bench-pressing iron bars instead of flexing your muscles in public."

"Why, you meddling little b—"

"Hugh? What's going on, sweetheart?"

Roxanne Wilmer surged toward her husband who was towering over Amanda like a blond cloud of doom.

"This accountant has a mouth on her the size of Vamoose County," Hugh snarled. "She's trying to pin Sheila's death on me, just because I rent MacAdo Farm and had words with Sheila when she tried to hike up the price."

Roxanne's bland features puckered and her dark eyes glittered as she rounded on Amanda. "Leave my husband alone. I will not have you pointing an accusing finger at him. He's done nothing wrong."

Like hell he hadn't! He had been screwing around with Sheila MacAdo, and Roxanne was so blindly loyal to him that she couldn't see the truth. What a pity to love a man so devotedly that you're oblivious to his faults and failings. Amanda certainly wasn't going to make that same mistake again— not with Thorn, the big rat!

Amanda considered telling Roxanne about Huey-boy's infidelity, there and then. It would serve Huey right if *Roxanne* was the one who threw her cherry pie in his bronzed face.

After giving the matter more thought, Amanda decided to back off. She was simply in a bad mood because Velma had exposed Thorn's and Jenny's secret rendezvous— in Hazard Accounting Office, of all places. What a low blow!

When Amanda wheeled away from Huey's and Roxanne's threatening glowers, she came face-to-face with Jenny Long who was attractively dressed in her designer jeans and western shirt, holding a pan of mouthwatering cinnamon rolls to be entered in the baking contest.

"This is the thanks I get?" Amanda muttered bitterly. "I thought you said we were friends."

Jenny glanced sideways at Velma who was smacking her gum and frowning in disapproval. "It wasn't what Velma thought," she hastened to explain. "I swear it wasn't, Amanda. Nicky and I were just— "

"You're fired, Jenny," Amanda quickly cut in.

"Fine, I'm fired," Jenny replied, a mist of tears swimming in her vivid green eyes. "Go ahead and make the same mistake I made when I was seventeen. I didn't wait for Nicky to come back from basic training with the marines. I turned to somebody else who wasn't half the man Nicky is. I promise you that you'll be sorry if you break off with him because of this. He's the best thing going."

Amanda pivoted on her Justin boot heels and stamped off, still fuming. The day was turning out to be a total disaster.

Amanda propelled herself toward the canning booths, hoping that winning blue ribbons would compensate for having her heart ripped out by the taproot. She certainly needed something to boost her flagging spirits.

Royce Shirley was standing in front of a booth where the winners of the sewing competition were displayed. When he spotted Amanda, he took a long draw on his cigarette and smirked sardonically. "Dodged anymore bombs lately?"

Amanda pulled up short to watch Royce exhale a puff of smoke from his cigarette— the same brand she had found at the scene of the crime. "Pushed anymore estranged wives off any ladders lately?" she retaliated.

Like a nicotine-breathing dragon, Royce blew smoke in Amanda's face. "You're really asking for it, aren't you? I wish I was the one who planted the bomb on your porch."

"Who said it was on my porch?"

"That's the story circulating around Vamoose and Pronto. I didn't do it, by the way."

"Yeah, and the prisons are crammed full of innocent men. Nobody seems to want to accept responsibility for what they've done— you included."

Royce pointed his smoldering cigarette at Amanda as if it were an extra finger, and glared at her through narrowed blue eyes. "Because of you, I've been hounded to death with questions from patrons at my feed store. I've just about had enough of it."

"So what do you plan to do next? Douse me with pesticide?"

"Just back off before I lose my temper."

"Is that what you told Sheila?"

"As a matter of fact, I did." Royce pulled himself up to full stature, threw back his red head, and took another puff on his cigarette. "And don't forget how Sheila ended up— with her melon cracked and a picket fence post in her chest."

When Royce sauntered away to view the other fair booths, Amanda pretended his back was a target and she was hurling invisible darts at it. Now she was beginning to wonder if the green vehicle Harry Ogelbee and Thorn had swerved to miss was actually Royce's two-tone green Dodge truck. Who was to say for sure — in pouring rain or a cloud of dust— what make and model that green blur had been.

Frowning pensively, Amanda made her way to the vegetable booth. To her dismay, Doralee Muchmore's precisely packed green beans had won a blue ribbon. Amanda's entry was nowhere to be seen among the jars boasting red, yellow, and white ribbons, either.

When Amanda saw Lula MacAdo browsing through the row of booths she motioned to the elderly widow. "I don't see my green beans among the entries. Do you know what became of them?"

Lula tilted her gray head back to peer at the name tags through her bifocals. "Well, I don't know, sugar. I brought all the entries down here for the judges to inspect. Are your peaches in the fruit booth?"

"I haven't checked yet."

Side by side, Amanda and Lula strolled past the arts and crafts booths to survey the shelves of fruit. As usual, Lula's watermelon preserves had taken grand prize of all the canned goods. Roxanne Wilmer's jar of cherries had won a blue ribbon.

No one had even bothered to compete against Lula's watermelons and Roxanne's cherries. It would have been a waste of time.

Doralee's peaches boasted a red ribbon and Jenny Long's apricots boasted a yellow ribbon.

Amanda's peaches, swimming in their cloudy yellow syrup, were nowhere to be found.

"Well, that is odd," Lula said, staring through her bifocals. "All the entries had to be delivered to me to be listed and labeled. I brought all of these jars to the fair myself, except for Jenny's apricots. She delivered them to me while I was at the beauty shop. I can't imagine what the judges could have done with your jars, sugar. I'll be sure to question them after they finish up this afternoon."

Glumly, Amanda ambled off to survey the booth of baked goods. Her great expectations had tumbled to the toes of her boots. She thought she had Sheila's murder all figured out and now she wasn't so sure. She thought she and Thorn had no secrets from each other and that had turned out to be a bad joke. And furthermore, she hadn't received any ribbons for her canned goods. Hell's bells, her jars weren't even on the shelves with the other entries!

Amanda paused to watch the panel of judges affixing ribbons to the prizewinning baked goods. Roxanne Wilmer's cherry tarts had won grand champion. Jenny Long's cinnamon rolls had won a blue ribbon. Doralee Muchmore's blond-walnut brownies had taken a red ribbon.

Everybody around Vamoose and Pronto could have been one of Betty Crocker's cooking elves— except Amanda Hazard. She didn't have a green thumb, sewing talent, or a magic wand wooden spoon. Obviously she didn't have a domestic bone in her body.

"Hazard, I've got to talk to you."

Amanda jerked up her head at the sound of Thorn's low, sexy voice. At that same instant another sexy voice drawled over the loudspeaker, introducing Billy Jane Baxter and the Horseshoe Band. While Billie Jane crooned a tune about a woman done wrong, Amanda turned her back on Thorn.

"Go away and leave me alone. I'm having a bad day. I hold you partially responsible for it."

"Hazard, it wasn't what you think," Nick insisted as he trailed after her.

"Now there's an overused phrase," she muttered, reminding herself that these boots were made for walking— or so Nancy Sinatra's old song went.

Nick grabbed her arm and spun her around to face him. "It was nothing."

"It was *everything* and you blew it," Amanda blared at him.

When heads turned in synchronized rhythm to determine the cause of the outburst, Nick latched onto Hazard's upper arm and towed her away from the crowd. "We need to find someplace where we can talk."

"At a fair jam-packed with people?" Amanda scoffed.

Nick glanced around while Hazard tried to worm out of his grasp. When he spotted the carnival operator with bulging arms covered with tattoos unloading riders from the Ferris wheel, Nick hauled Hazard across the park.

"You call this private?" Amanda stared dubiously at Thorn and then glared at the tattooed man who was visually undressing her. The creep. "Plug your eyes back in their sockets, buster, and pay attention to your business. In my opinion— "

Before Hazard launched into one of her opinionated spiels, Nick shoveled her onto the padded seat. "Don't take your frustrations out on the rest of the world."

"Why not? You take your lust out on anything in a skirt."

"I do not!" Nick all but yelled.

The engine sputtered and the suspended seat rocked as it ascended the Ferris wheel. It was only then that Amanda remembered she had an aversion to heights. Thorn, the sneaky rascal, obviously recalled she didn't function as well at elevated heights. He was obviously planning to keep her stranded atop the Ferris wheel while he presented his excuse for the kiss he shared with Jenny.

Twisting sideways, Nick laid his arm over the back of the seat and met Hazard's glittering baby blues. "Now look, Hazard. Velma completely misread the situation at your office. It was nothing more than old acquaintances reestablishing a friendship. It was just a peace-treaty kiss and hug."

"There was a hug, too?" Amanda scowled as she watched the bystanders on the ground shrink more with each lurch of the Ferris wheel. "Geez, Thorn, couldn't you at least have had the decency to make out somewhere besides the office where *I* pay the bills? You really take the cake! The tryst was literally on me. I hope the air conditioning was working properly. Hate for the two of you to work up a sweat!"

"Damn it, Hazard," Nick growled. "I actually *did* take the cake— your lopsided German chocolate, to be specific. It cost me twenty-five bucks to keep it off the auction block so the whole damned town wouldn't laugh themselves sick when they got a look at the thing. And as for your canned goods, they're sitting under the skirted tables of the booths. The beans and peaches obviously didn't seal properly. You didn't leave them long enough in the pressure cooker, is my guess. The beans are fizzing with so many germs carrying botulism that you could wipe out the population of Vamoose in one meal. Your peaches have so much mold in them that they turned green."

Amanda was so mortified she wanted to bawl her head off. She would have, too, if the jerking motion of the elevated seat hadn't lodged the tears in the back of her eyes.

"I got here early to pay for your cake before it even arrived and I stashed the jars out of sight," Nick informed her as the seat lurched onto the tip-top of the Ferris wheel. "And do you know why I did it, Hazard?"

Amanda gulped and told herself not to look down. "Why, Thorn?"

"Because I care about you, damn it. Just you. And for your information this is the kind of kiss I planted on my friend Jen's lips." He leaned over to press his sensuous lips lightly against hers. "And *this* is the way I kiss you, just in case you've forgotten . . ."

Amanda swore the bottom had dropped out of the seat when Thorn got down to the steamy business of kissing her breathless. It felt as if a volcanic explosion was erupting inside her. Thorn was definitely high voltage, Amanda thought, dazed.

When Amanda returned to her senses, she heard the sound of applause from the ground far below. Jenny Long was smiling up at her—with both thumbs up. Velma, her dyed red head tipped upward, was high-fiving with Bubba Jr. who was cradled in his father's bulky arms.

"There. You see? Everybody in Vamoose and

Pronto approves," Nick murmured as he raised his ruffled raven head. "You're not my huckleberry, Hazard. You're my bowl of *cherries.*"

Cherries . . . The word rang in Amanda's ears. As the Ferris wheel made its descent, Amanda stared across the fairgrounds and parking lot from her bird's eye view. Her gaze focused on Roxanne Wilmer who was striding toward her . . . Johnsongrass-green Pontiac Grand Prix.

Holy smoke!

Suddenly, the scene of the crime flashed into Amanda's mind with vivid clarity. Every time she had walked into Lula MacAdo's alphabetically arranged kitchen Amanda had been stung by the nagging feeling that she had overlooked an important clue. And she had! It had been the jar of *cherries* that had been out of alphabetical order on Lula's window sill. Doralee hadn't delivered the cherries, as Amanda had mistakenly presumed. Roxanne had!

The cherries had been sitting between Doralee's green beans and peaches. Lula had placed Doralee's beans and peaches in front of her own watermelon preserves— in perfect alphabetical order. And in the dazed blur the week had become after Sheila's fatal fall, Lula had been too preoccupied to question Roxanne's jar of cherries in the line up on the windowsill.

No one had circled back to do Sheila in, Amanda realized. Roxanne had arrived after Lula left for her hair appointment and errands. The Cherry Queen of Pronto had shown up while Sis Hix was at her doctor's appointment and before Joe Wahkinney stopped by. Roxanne had added her jar of fruit to the line of canned goods on the window sill.

Roxanne Wilmer was the last person to see Sheila alive. She had shoved Sheila off the ladder and covered her tracks with the rake.

The only thing Amanda didn't know was why Roxanne had circled back to swipe the billfold and remove a photo. A photo of what?

"I've got to get off this thing!" Amanda hollered at Mr. Tattoo.

As the seat rocked to and fro, Amanda pulled her legs beneath her, squatting into a crouch.

"Hazard? What the sweet loving hell are you doing? Trying to commit suicide?" Thorn croaked.

"I'm cutting to the chase." Amanda hurled herself off the seat when it came within jumping distance of the ground.

Thorn made an unsuccessful attempt to grab Hazard by her belt, but he came up holding nothing but air. "Am I back in your good graces or aren't I?" he called as Hazard hit the ground running.

Amanda didn't have time to reply. She had a clever murderer to apprehend. With no time to spare, Amanda zigzagged through the crowd. Roxanne had just plopped down on her car seat when Amanda dashed into the parking lot, her arms flapping like an airborne duck.

"You're under arrest!" Amanda yelled breathlessly. "Hold it right there, Roxanne."

Obviously Roxanne realized Amanda had finally gotten all her facts straight and arrived at the fatal conclusion. Roxanne mashed on the accelerator, spitting gravel.

It occurred to Amanda, a second too late, that Roxanne intended to back over her—in the pretense of an accident. Amanda made a wild dive the instant before the rear bumper of Roxanne's Grand Prix flattened her like a shadow.

A dull groan tumbled from Amanda's lips as she skidded across the graveled parking lot and smacked her head against the fender of Thorn's black truck. A fuzzy haze fogged Amanda's senses as Roxanne slammed the car into drive and launched off like a patriot missile.

"Hazard!" Thorn's booming voice infiltrated Amanda's jumbled thoughts. Her head throbbing, Amanda rolled to her back to see two fuzzy images of Thorn kneeling beside her.

Nick didn't bother asking if Hazard was okay. He could damned well tell that she wasn't. There was a bump the size of a chicken egg between her dilated eyes. Frayed fabric on the shoulder seam of her blouse exposed scraped and bleeding flesh. There were holes in the knees of her Rocky Mountain jeans.

"Roxanne shoved Sheila," Amanda got out shakily. "Track her down, Thorn. I'll stay here and throw up."

Nick bounded to his feet while Hazard lost her breakfast. Concussion, he quickly diagnosed.

"Hang on, Hazard. I'll have somebody here to help you in a minute."

Amanda heaved a sickening breath and stared up at the brawny silhouette in blue jeans and chambray shirt that eclipsed the sun like an awe-inspiring hero from the Old West.

"Thorn?"

"Yeah, Hazard?"

"You're my bowl of cherries, too. . . . And you can tell Jenny she's re-hired . . ."

With a relieved smile, Thorn wheeled around and raced away.

Amanda slumped on the gravel to toss a few more cookies. And then the world turned a hazy shade of black.

Amanda awakened a couple of hours later to see Dr. Simm's familiar face and teasing smile against a background of sterile stainless steel and white hospital walls.

"I've reserved space for you, Amanda," Dr. Simms cheerfully announced. "You're becoming a regular around here." His Reeboks squeaked as he stepped closer to fluff the pillow behind her bandaged head. "Didn't break your arm or lose your hearing this time, though. I wonder how many of your nine lives you have left."

"I want to go home," Amanda pouted.

"Well, tough," he said good-naturedly. "You're booked for overnight."

"I don't want to be booked overnight."

"Then don't hit your head on heavy-duty steel bumpers next time you make a spectacular swan-dive into the gravel. Your grand finale acrobatics earned you a ringside seat at my circus, and I make the rules here."

"Lucky thing you're a doctor," Amanda grumbled crabbily. "You'd make a lousy comedian."

The chuckling Dr. Simms and his squeaky Reeboks were making an exit when Thorn arrived. "Is Hazard going to be all right?"

Dr. Simms glanced back at his hostile patient. "It is my professional opinion that she'll be fine, but I'm keeping her until tomorrow morning. You planning to stay the night?"

Nick nodded.

"I'll have one of the nurses bring you a cot when visiting hours are over," he said before he squeaked off.

"Well?" Amanda demanded as Thorn approached her bed. "Was I right again or was I right?"

Nick grimaced and scowled at the gloating question. "You were right, Hazard," he managed to choke out. "I gave Roxanne my rabid-dog cop routine at the police station. She broke down and confessed all. Seems that she knew all about Hugh's affair with Sheila, just like she knew about his torrid affair with the late Sally Marie Taylor. Roxanne was the one who sneaked into the house and doctored Sally Marie's vodka with those high-powered migraine tablets. Roxanne was also the one who shoved Sheila when she was provoked too far by threats and insults."

"Just as I thought," Amanda inserted proudly.

Nick ignored the comment and continued. "According to Roxanne, she warned Sheila to keep her hands off Hugh. Sheila smirked and called Roxanne a brown paper bag, right to her face."

"Sheila must have been an expert at cheap shots. It's a wonder she got away with them as long as she did."

Nick nodded in agreement. "Sheila made the mistake of telling Roxanne that she carried a picture of her and Hugh in the sack, stark naked. Sheila threatened to flash it all over town if Roxanne tried to interfere.

"Sheila always thought she could do whatever she wanted to do with whomever she chose to do it, without facing the consequences. Roxanne proved her wrong."

"I suppose Roxanne only had time to check for Sheila's pulse and rake the footprints out of the garden before she spotted the arrival of Joe Wahkinney."

Nick nodded his dark head. "After Joe came and left, Roxanne doubled back to get the wallet and remove the obscene picture. She saw dust billowing on the road again and took off before you arrived on the scene. Roxanne was returning the billfold the day Harry Ogelbee nearly rammed her broadside at the blind intersection—"

"And she was speeding away from my house after she planted the homemade bomb, causing

you to swerve into the ditch," Amanda finished
for him. "I must have really upset Roxanne after
I managed to instigate the fight between Huey
and Royce at the ice cream social."

"Yep," Nick confirmed. "She held you personally responsible for Hugh's black eye and
split lip. She intended to ruin your good looks—
at the very least—by concocting a liquid bomb
made from a volatile combination of household
cleansers. From all indication Roxanne worships
the ground Hugh floats over because she con-
siders him as beautiful as she is plain. Roxanne
is fanatically protective and possessive—"

"To the point of disposing of anyone who
poses a threat to her marriage to the Viking-god
cowboy," Amanda added. "Can you imagine a
woman actually killing to protect her man from
other women?"

"Can you imagine a woman breaking off a
perfectly good relationship because of a harmless kiss and hug between old friends who have
no romantic interest in each other?" Nick strategically questioned.

Amanda glanced up at Thorn's smiling
bronzed face and appraised his striking masculine physique. "Said woman would have to be
just plain stupid to botch up a perfectly good
relationship because of a platonic kiss, wouldn't
she?"

"Yep."

"Thorn, would you call Mother and tell her
we can't make it to the Hazard Labor Day picnic

tonight? I don't think I feel up to watching you being roasted over an open pit."

"I already did, Hazard." Nick walked over to close and lock the door.

"What are you doing, Thorn?" Amanda bleated when he sank down on the side of the bed to doff his boots and peel off his shirt. "We're in a hospital, for Pete's sake!"

"Ever done it in a hospital, Hazard?"

"Never."

"Me, either. I'm feeling spontaneous again . . ."

He was also feeling extremely aroused, Amanda noted when Thorn rolled over and gathered her into his sinewy arms. Now this, Amanda decided, was a sure cure for a headache.

Okay, so she wasn't Vamoose's greatest cook. But she could sniff out clues with the best of them. And she obviously had something this sexy country cop appreciated.

As Jenny had said: Only an idiot would give up on Nick Thorn. He was definitely the best thing going . . . and he wasn't bad coming, either.

"Dr. Thorn?" Amanda purred playfully.

"Yeah, Hazard?" Thorn growled back.

"Is that your thermometer?"

Thorn's pearly whites gleamed in the scant light. "If you say so, Hazard."

Amanda smiled to herself. Although she hadn't received blue ribbons for all her aches, efforts, and pains, she had successfully solved another

case in Vamoose. And who needed a measly ribbon when she had Thorn for her grand prize?

Amanda's low opinion of hospitals was im-
proving by the minute. Thorn was much more
thorough than a practicing physician.

Now *this* was a physical examination to write
home about. . . . But not, of course, to Mother.

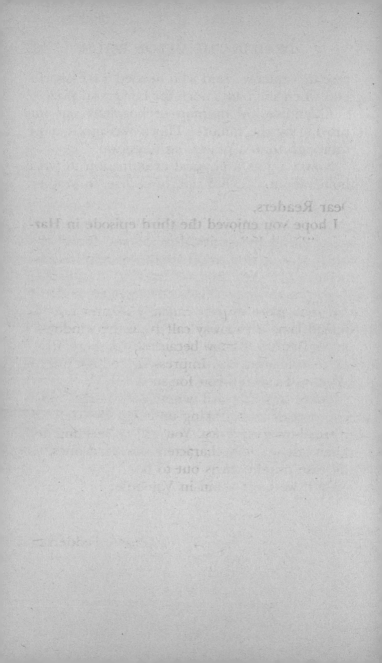

Dear Readers,

I hope you enjoyed the third episode in Hazard's "Dead In" series. In case you found the incident of roping a calf from a pickup window farfetched, let me assure you that it *is* possible. In fact, I patterned the scene after an incident that took place on our ranch. Husband Ed did indeed lasso a runaway calf from the window— on his first try. I know because I was there, driving the pickup truck. Impressed the heck out of me, too, I can tell you for sure!

Please join Hazard when she returns with Thorn at her side, taking up where they left off in small-town America. You will be meeting another cast of lively characters— or dead ones, as the case usually turns out to be.

Until we meet again in Vamoose.

Connie Feddersen

WHO DUNNIT? JUST TRY AND FIGURE IT OUT!

THE MYSTERIES OF MARY ROBERTS RINEHART

THE AFTER HOUSE	(2821-0, $3.50/$4.50)
THE ALBUM	(2334-0, $3.50/$4.50)
ALIBI FOR ISRAEL AND OTHER STORIES	(2764-8, $3.50/$4.50)
THE BAT	(2627-7, $3.50/$4.50)
THE CASE OF JENNIE BRICE	(2193-3, $2.95/$3.95)
THE CIRCULAR STAIRCASE	(3528-4, $3.95/$4.95)
THE CONFESSION AND SIGHT UNSEEN	(2707-9, $3.50/$4.50)
THE DOOR	(1895-5, $3.50/$4.50)
EPISODE OF THE WANDERING KNIFE	(2874-1, $3.50/$4.50)
THE FRIGHTENED WIFE	(3494-6, $3.95/$4.95)
THE GREAT MISTAKE	(2122-4, $3.50/$4.50)
THE HAUNTED LADY	(3680-9, $3.95/$4.95)
A LIGHT IN THE WINDOW	(1952-1, $3.50/$4.50)
LOST ECSTASY	(1791-X, $3.50/$4.50)
THE MAN IN LOWER TEN	(3104-1, $3.50/$4.50)
MISS PINKERTON	(1847-9, $3.50/$4.50)
THE RED LAMP	(2017-1, $3.50/$4.95)
THE STATE V. ELINOR NORTON	(2412-6, $3.50/$4.50)
THE SWIMMING POOL	(3679-5, $3.95/$4.95)
THE WALL	(2560-2, $3.50/$4.50)
THE YELLOW ROOM	(3493-8, $3.95/$4.95)